The Risks We Take For Love

By: Leigh Ann

This is a work of fiction. Unless otherwise indicated, all the names, characters, businesses, places, events and incidents in this book are either the product of the author's imagination or used in a fictitious manner. Any resemblance to actual persons, living or dead, or actual events is purely coincidental.

ISBN: 9798362213695

Contact -Crystell Publications
PO BOX 8044 / Edmond – OK 73083
www.crystellpublications.com
(405) 414-3991

Printed in the USA

Dedication

I Dedicated My first Book to my Mama, Thank You For always Being My Rock You Pushed me to Greatness. You Always Told ME I would Be Great and That I Could Do Anything I Put My Mind To. I'm forever thankful for everything you do. No Matter What Your always right behind me. I Love You Forever.
Love always your Favorite Daughter

Acknowledgments

First, I would like to acknowledge My lord And Savior Jesus Christ, without his Grace and Mercy, none of this would be possible. My kids who are my motivation to push for greatness. My family for being there for me through this whole process, from reading samples to helping me decide to publish Independent. I appreciate all the support. To My Man, My Partner, My Best Friend Dairus thank you for believing in me and supporting every dream and idea I have , no matter how big or small. Always telling me you can do it. You made me be a better version of me and I'm forever grateful for everything you did to make this possible.

Enjoy This Play List While You Read

So, won't you say my name, say my name?
If you claim you want me, it ain't no thang.
You're acting kinda shady,
You ain't been calling me baby.
Boy, you can go and stop playing games,
Playing games
-Summer Walker

CHAPTER 1

It had to be the *hottest* day of the summer. It was about a hundred degrees outside, but it didn't matter, the block was jumping. Everyone was sitting on the porch watching all the block boys try to open the fire hydrant for the little kids. They were out today no matter how hot it was.

I was going get one of them, too. "Bianca, why don't you and your li'l home girls go play or some shit?" I asked, snapping at my little sister. She was irritating as hell.

To prove it, she scoffed, "Girl, bye. You not my mama, and I'm sixteen years old. The fuck you mean 'go play'?" Bianca snapped back, rolling her eyes.

"She the closest thing to it, so watch your mouth!" my other sister Brazil chimed in.

The sixteen-year-old's face twisted further. "Man, y'all get on my nerves, y'all just want us to leave so y'all can be some hoes!"

"PERIOD, Sis. Now get the fuck on!" I yelled at her. She ain't need to be sitting out here with us anyway. Something was bound to pop off, and me and Brazil tried our best to keep our baby sister away from all the shit the hood had to offer.

Our mama wasn't shit, she had three daughters and didn't give a fuck about us at all. I mean, she made sure we ate and had a roof over our head, but as soon as I was about sixteen, Brazil was about thirteen, and our baby sister Bianca was seven, Mama busted out with her boyfriend and left me in charge.

I cried, wondering how I was going to take care of us. Mama's last words before she walked out was "Don't let everything I worked hard for go to waste. This was my mama's house, so you better keep it up and you better make sure your sisters are straight. I don't want CPS looking for me."

"Ma! What I'm supposed to do for money?!"

"You better use what God gave you. See, that piece of gold between your legs can make you all the money you need if you use it right." With that, she slammed the door behind her. I'll never forget holding my baby sister that night as she cried for our mama.

"Brittany. *Brittany.* BRITTANY!" Bianca yelled, snapping me out of my flashback

What Girl, I thought we told u to beat it"

"Give me some money me n Kimmy Gone walk to the center to go swim "

"HERE" I handed her a $20 bill now bye! And you better wash the dishes when u get back, you going work for this money "

“Like you do shaking ass every night “said Bianca as she bent over and twerked her ass

“Watch your mouth Bianca n stop before i beat you ass “ Brazil Yelled she hated how ghetto and loud Bianca was I think it was because she reminded her to much of our mama , Bianca Looked and acted just like Mama and it drove Zil Crazy.

Zil was the polite and quite one out of us now don’t get me wrong she will pop off if need be but Zil stayed to herself, went to school chilled with her Lil boyfriend and did hair at the shop. She was one of the baddest in the D with that hair shit. Zil did every dancer I worked with weave. Yea that’s right Iam a dancer I had to make money and fast after mama left so I went to ACE OF SPADES on 8mile for amateur Night on Thursday made a check and it’s been on ever since .

I was the hottest bitch in there, Brown skin about 5”4 a small waist and a big ass. My hair hung long to the middle of my back and my skin was flawless not to mention i could dance my ass off ... At first i was shy about stripping but now i was gettin booked for party’s at least 4 nights out the week, the money was good and i could take care if my sisters that was what was most important to me. My mama had let us down and i wasn’t about too.

“Be Home Before dark Bianca, don’t make me come looking for you” Zil yelled down the street as Bianca and Her friend walked way

My cell phone was ringing nonstop, i already knew who it was. After the like 9th call i answered “WHAT XAZIER “

“DAMN YOU STILL MAD B”

“YES, IM MAD I HEARD YOU BEEN BACK FUCKING WITH KRYSTAL AGAIN “

"Man, I wasn't fucking with her B I Stopped by to see my daughter "

"BOY" I said rolling my eyes like he could see me "You pocket dial me , I heard y'all fuckin "

"Brittany i wasn't fucking her I swear Man You Know Keem fuck with her sister that was him fucking he had my phone "

He really tried to use that high school ass lie on me. Like, why did that grown-ass man have your phone and where were you while he had it? I was so over playing games with his ass. "What*ever,* Zay. We been goin' back an' forth about you and her for years. I'm over it," and I was about to hang up on him, but suddenly, he was standing in front of me. Damn, he was fine. "Zay. What do you want?!"

"You, B! You know I love you, girl. I miss you!"

I sneered at him. "Whatever, Zay, I'm sick of your lying ass, and I'm sick of you and Krystal. I'm just over it now, go on," I said, pushing him out my face.

"B, stop playing with me! You can't be over *this."* Then, he leans in to kiss me, parting my lips with his tongue. As soon as I felt his lips on mine, I forgot why I was mad. I love Zay, he has a hold of my heart.

Still, I swear I hated that I loved his cheating ass. When my mama left for the first couple months, Zay held it down. He paid all the bills and kept food on the table. 'Til I started dancing, at least. Zay hated the fact that I danced, but hell, Zil and Bianca were my responsibility. I couldn't let them see me struggle, so I did what I had to do.

Zay always said he had enough money to take care of me for the rest of my life, but I wanted to make it on my own I want to my sisters to learn that at any time, I could give up on them and they'd have nothing left. Anyone could. I learned that when Mama left.

Either way, I love to make my own money and being able to take care of my responsibilities. I made sure my sisters had anything they needed. I would teach them to be independent. Don't never put all your eggs in one basket, don't ever depend on anyone to take care of you, no matter who it is. Not your mama, not your daddy, maybe not even me.

As Zay's tongue danced with mine, all the anger I had towards him went away. I instantly got wet. I had missed him, and yeah, it only been a week, but it felt like forever. He slipped his hand under my skirt, moving my thong to the side so he could caress my opening. I shivered. "Damn, B, you that wet for me? I thought you was mad?"

I mumbled against his lips, "Hush, I'm—"

"Y'all is *OUTSIDE,"* I heard Zil snap at the two of us. It broke me from the trance Zay had over me.

I forgot my sister was right there and that we were indeed outside for the most part. "My bad, Zil, but it was just a kiss. Don't act like you ain't never kissed before."

Her nose wrinkled. "Yeah, I have, but not in front of you or the whole block, and I damn sure ain't letting nobody put they hand up my skirt!" she scoffed, rolling her eyes.

Fixing my skirt while blushing, I clapped back with, "Grow up, Zil. You do too much!" Then I walked in the house with Zay right behind me. In fact, he followed me all the way up the stairs and to my room.

As I sat on my bed, he walked closer, taking off his black Fitted and placing his gun on my nightstand. Zay grabbed a handful of my hair and pulled me in for a kiss. The moment our lips touched, I felt a chill over my body. It's crazy he could have that effect on me.

Yes, I was mad at him, and yes, I knew he was lying about fucking Krystal a week ago, but it's like I could never be mad at him for too long. He has a hold on my mind, body, and soul. Zay was my first love. We been together on and off for about five years.

As we kissed, he pulled my cami over my head and my breasts fell free. His fingers delicately played over my nipple as he continued to kiss me, and a soft moan left my lips. Then, he began to suck on the right bud as he flicked the left one and I felt my back arch as he kissed down my stomach on his way to pull my skirt up. There, he began removing my thong with his teeth, grabbing them and putting them in his pocket.

"Zay, no, I just got those—" I whined.

He smirked. "Shut up, I love the way she smells. I'mma save it for later." Zay's tongue flicking along my pearl. Slowly licking and rubbing my inner thigh at the same time, he began eating me like it was his last meal. My body was shaking and soon, I was climaxing. Afterwards, he sucked all my juices up.

I reached down and blindly unbuckled his jean shorts while he stepped out of them, and then his boxers. I got up, pushed him down on the bed and saddled him, grinding my hips on him, feeling him grow, but not letting him into my opening yet. I took the smooth head and rubbed up and down my slit before letting him enter me. With a breathless groan, I grinded and rolled my hips as he pushed deep inside me, and our rhythm was perfectly in sync.

Zay flipped me over and entered me from behind as I threw it back on him, dancing to a beat in my head. The harder he pounded me, the faster I threw my ass back. "Fuck, B!" he yelled out as he filled me up. We laid there, trying to catch our breath.

See, this is my problem—I can't stop having sex with Zay, and once we *do* have sex, the problems we have just fade away. I needed to get away from him, unless I wanted to continue to get cheated on and hurt. But hell, who was I to judge? I did my dirt too, but only when we weren't together.

His phone had been ringing the whole time. "Aye, B. I'm gone," he suddenly informed while getting up off the bed and putting his clothes on.

My eyes went wide, but to be honest, I wasn't surprised in the slightest. This was typical. "For real, Zay, that's all you wanted? I was thinking we could chill or hit the mall!" I frowned while watching him put his gun in his waistband.

He just shook his head, laughing like it was going to make things any better. "Now B, you know I can't chill. It's the first an' I'm 'bout to hit the road in a few, I got money to make. I'll be back in town in a few days, maybe we can do something then."

I rolled my eyes and sighed, "Whatever, I got to work anyway," I mumbled as he walked out of my room, leaving me there lost in my thoughts.

I was *over* this nigga. I swear, I just couldn't seem to shake his ass. I'm so sick of playing games. One day I'm going to leave his ass for good, find me a man just for me, get up out this hood, and never look back. I had some money I had been saving so I could move me and my sisters to Cali, and soon I would have enough so we could get the fuck on... If I could just stay out that damn mall and jewelry store.

I got up from my king-size pillow top bed, wishing I could lay there all day, but I had to get ready for work. I was working day shift at Hardbody and then afterwards I had a party at AOS. It was summer, so bar season was slow. I had to work two bars a day if I wanted to keep up with the lifestyle, I had become adapted to.

Now, don't get me wrong, we still lived in the hood in Southwest Detroit—a four bedroom, with two bathrooms. From the outside, it looked like your average house in the hood, but I made sure we had the best of the best furniture and appliances. I even redid the bathrooms about two years ago. It was a simple job, and I planned on knocking out a wall and remodeling the kitchen in the next few months.

I was never going to let my sisters suffer because of what our mom did to us. They always talked about having a nice home and the best things in life when we were little, and Mama made all those kinds of promises. She would tell us that all the working and tricking she was doing was going to get us out of the hood.

For a while, I could tell that mom had us in her best interests, but then she met Jake. She quit working a real job, and a starred tricking full time for him. That's when everything went downhill, from rarely staying home to never cooking dinner for us at night, she'd even stopped going to the school and checking on our grades. Most surprising of all, she quit doing Bianca hair, and Mom was a hairdresser, that's where Brazil learned how to do hair.

Mama started to look skinny and tired in the face. Word on the street was that she was getting high; I kind of could tell too, she wasn't buying us nice clothes or doing any of the typical 'Mom' things. This was going on for about two years before she left, I should've known then. It was all about Jake from then on out, he came into Mama's life and turned it upside down. Mama was never like this, Daddy died a little after Bianca was born and she took a nosedive. She met Jake, and the rest was history.

I walked in the bathroom to take a shower. After stepping into the tub, I turned the shower on as hot as it could go and stepped in, just letting the water run down my body. Grabbing the Dove lavender bar, I started washing up. After getting out, I dried off and brushed my long, curly hair into a neat bun, put on my lash strips, and applied a little lip gloss over my full lips.

Walking out of the bathroom and into my walk-in closet, I started fingering through my clothes, looking for something to put on. I decided on a terrycloth two-piece light pink short and top set with my all-white VaporMax. I was going to work anyway, no need to do too much.

All dressed up and ready to go, I walked back outside to find Zil yelling into her phone at Bianca. "Bianca, why Mrs. Laran calling talking 'bout she just put you out her house 'cause she caught you downstairs kissing her grandson?" I rolled my eyes, 'cause I knew where this was heading, and I didn't have time for it to today.

Although we tried our hardest to protect Bianca from the hood, she somehow found a way to be the biggest hood rat around. She didn't even go to school out here like some kids did, but that didn't stop her from engaging in all hood activities. Brazil yelled in her phone at Bianca, but I just shook my head as I walked to my all-black 2020 Durango, hopped in, turned the radio up and headed to work. I would let Brazil deal with Bianca, I wasn't in the mood today.

Same group of bitches, ain't no adding to the picture
Drop a couple racks, watch this ass get bigger
Drinkin' on liquor, and I'm lookin' at your nigga
If his money right, he can eat it like a Snickers

I ain't got time for you fake-ass hoes
Talkin' all loud in them fake-ass clothes
Fake-ass shoes match their fake-ass gold
I'm the realest bitch ever to you snake-ass hoes

- *City Girls*

CHAPTER 2

BIANCA

I was so sick of Zil and Brit telling me what to do, man. I had two more years, then I would be grown, and I could move the fuck away from them. They thought I was the same crybaby little girl I was when Mama left, but I wasn't. To tell the truth, Mama leaving made me the strong, outspoken boss bitch I was today. I understood they wanted what was best for me, but damn, they could let me live! I already couldn't go to school with my friends; they had me in some private school in Taylor, away from everybody I grew up with. Brit and Zil tried to keep me away from the hood, but what they didn't know was that I *am* the hood.

Zil was yelling at me through the phone, telling me to make my way back to the block. I was just holding the phone, not paying any attention to what she was saying. Mrs. Laran came home early and caught me and my best friend Kimmy in the basement with her grandson and nephew.

We weren't doing anything—well, not yet anyway—but she flipped and called Zil on me, and now I'd have to deal with that bullshit when I got home. "Kim, can I stay over at your house tonight? I don't feel like dealing with my sisters when I get home," I sighed.

"Sure, my mama and auntie gone OT, so it's whatever," she agreed, looking down at her phone. I would have to ask Brit, because Zil wasn't having it. Zil was so hard on me.

She was so lame, and all she did was work, never had any fun, and she was so stuck up. You would never know we were sisters; we act totally different. I sent Brit a text.

It read, *'Can I stay at Kimmy's tonight? Your sister's tripping and I don't feel like dealing with that. I wasn't even doin' nothin' when Mrs. Laran came home. I know I was supposed to be at the pool, but we made a stop there first. Please, Brittany, PLEASE!'*

Quickly, a reply flashed over my screen. *'Girl, if you ain't go to the pool where my money?'* Then, *'I guess, but Zil gon' be on your ass, and I don't feel like all that, so just tell her before she be looking for you, and keep your li'l hot ass out that lady's house.'*

I typed back "Thanks, Sissy," with a winking emoji.

As me and Kimmy walked toward her house, we stopped at the store at the corner where there were a few guys shooting dice. One of the guys was me and Kimmy's other best friend Carlos. We had all grown up together since we were kids, and we were in the same class, until my sisters took me out and put me in that private school, of course.

"Bebe an' Kim, my two fave chicks!" Carlos cooed, placing his arm around us both.

We responded in unison. "Hey Los."

"Where y'all goin'?"

Kim glanced at him, then at the three guys he had with him. "To my house, y'all tryin' to come?" She pointed to the group of friends.

Carlos hung his head dramatically. "Mannn, who gonna be there for me?"

"I can call Tae-Tae, she was just asking about you," I suggested.

He grinned at the sound of that. "Oh, yeah, call her, I miss her big booty ass." We laughed as we all walked a few more blocks to Kimmy's place. Her mama and auntie were never in town, they were always on those casino bus trips, so Kim's house was where we all hung out. It was the only time I got to see my boyfriend, Marcus. As soon as we got to Kim's house, I sat on her porch and sent Marcus a text. *Hey, Baby. I'm staying at Kimmy's tonight.*

Soon my phone buzzed with his response, *St8 I'm on my way,* so I shot back with *Hurry up, I miss you and so do she.* I hadn't seen Marcus in two weeks at this point. My sister was on *bullshit* trying to have me locked down. They swore they wanted what was best for me, but locking me up in that house or watching my every move wasn't going to help.

I mean, they kept me on a short leash, but I still managed to go out, party, and fuck Marcus whenever I wanted to. My sisters thought I was still a virgin. Zil would lose it if she found out I had given it up two years ago, when I was fourteen. I couldn't believe she still was holding on to hers. If she knew what was good for her, she would get her some. Maybe then she wouldn't be so stuck up and uptight.

Kim asked me, "What you smiling for?"

"'Cause Marcus on his way, bitch. I need to get ready!"

She snickered. "Girl, you can get ready in my mama's room, I'm 'bout to smoke with Los and them. I called Tae-Tae, so she will be here in a li'l, then I'mma try to have Los put me on his friend..." Kimmy purred that last part, pointing to one of the boys who walked with us from the store.

"You a hoe," I noted, watching Kimmy lick her lips like she was undressing Carlos' boy with her eyes.

She broke her firm gaze to raise her eyebrow at me. "So, bitch? You act like you wasn't just in the basement kissing on Dan before his grandma came home!" Kim was laughing.

"So, bitch?" I parroted as I walked into the house to shower and get ready. I had a bag of clothes I kept over at Kimmy's house that I could use to change whenever I got away from my sisters, so I grabbed it on my way to the bathroom. I jumped in the shower and washed up as quickly as I could. I had to hurry; I knew Marcus wouldn't be long.

I got out of the shower and flipped through my bag for something to put on. Following some consideration, I grabbed a pair of white biker shorts and pulled them over my thick thighs and round ass. Then, I slipped a red tube top on, which sat right above my belly button, and I pulled my wet hair in a low ponytail. I didn't have my makeup bag, so I just put on some lip gloss. Two sprays of Marc Jacobs' Daisy perfume, and I was ready to see my man.

I went and sat on the porch with everybody and waited for my man to come. We smoked three blunts and had just started drinking when I saw Marcus walking up the block. He was fine, light-skinned with green eyes. You could see his waves booming from a mile away. He strutted up to the porch and picked me up off of last step, then he sat down and placed me on his lap.

He revealed a blunt and lit it, pulled from it two times and kissed me, blowing smoke in my mouth. I inhaled it and blew it out. From there, he passed the 'gas to Los, grabbed my cup of Patron, and began to drink from it. We all sat on the porch, getting high and drinking.

Two hours later, I was nice and buzzed. Feeling good. I looked around, and the crowd was smaller than it was before. I stood up and walked up the porch with Marcus right behind. As I passed by her, I tapped Kimmy's arm. She was sitting on Los' friend's lap in a chair. "I'm 'bout to go lay down. I'm high,"

She nodded. "Okay. You can go in my room, I'm gonna sleep in my mama's room."

"Bet," I called back as I walked in her house and downstairs to the basement where Kimmy's room was. I sat on her bed, but Marcus picked me up. My legs immediately wrapped around his waist and my arms circled around his neck.

He pushed my back up against the wall and kissed me while gripping my ass with both palms. "Damn, Bebe. You ain't got no panties on?" he asked.

"Nope," I said as I kissed on his neck.

He reached between my thighs. "Is that pussy wet?"

I whispered in his ear, "Touch it and see." Me and Marcus waste no time getting down to business. He really didn't talk much about anything but sex. Yeah, he was my boyfriend and all, but all we really did was smoke, drink, and fuck.

I felt his rough hand pulling my shorts down. Marcus laid me on the bed and tugged them all the way off, before taking his hand and slipping it under my shirt to rub my nipple.

His fingers pushed into my slit while his thumb circled around my clit, flicking and rubbing. I felt my juices running down his hand... He pulled the digits out and put them to my lips. I took his fingers in my mouth and sucked my sweet nectar off of them. Kisses were trailed down my stomach until he reached my opening, and his tongue slipped inside as he began to eat me up and play with my nipples at the same time.

I was about to cum; I couldn't control myself. I began to shake as I climaxed in his mouth. Before I could reorient myself, he moved up and slipped inside of me "Unhh, Marcus!" I cried as he pumped faster and faster. Suddenly, he pulled out and turned me over. Following suit, I got up on all fours so he could enter with no problems. He grinded my slit open slowly until I began to throw it back at a rapid tempo, clapping our hips together.

I knew he wasn't going to last long with how my ass was slapping back into his lap. "Damn, Bebe, chill! I ain't ready to cum," he whispered in my ear, but I ignored him and continued to fuck him back. His arm wrapped around my neck to choke me from behind as he pounded harder and faster. I felt him twitch inside of me, and then his body went limp. We continued like this throughout the night, because who knew when I would be able to see him again?

"Bianca? Bianca. *Bianca.*"

I felt Marcus shaking me out my sleep. "What?!" I snapped. I hate being woke up, and I knew I was gonna have a hangover. I opened my eyes a little bit and peeked at him, squinting.

"Man, it's twelve, I'm 'bout to dip, I got some shit I need to take care of."

Grabbing his arm, I pulled him closer, so he wrapped me up and kissed me deep. "Aww, Bae, I don't want you to leave," I said in between kissing him on his lips over and over.

His arms squeezed around me. "I know, but I got to go make me some money, Bebe. See if your sisters will let you stay over here another night and I'll be back." He kissed me again, walked up the stairs, and then he was gone.

It was going be hard to get my sisters to let me stay out again, but I was going to think of something. I *love* spending time with Marcus. We had been together about a year now, and he was like two years older than me. Yeah, I know what you're thinking: wasn't I just kissing another guy not less than twenty-four hours ago?

I was, but that doesn't mean I didn't love Marcus. He vibe good as hell, and he was so nice to me. Anything I wanted, he would get for me. I hated that I didn't get to see him like I wanted to, but I was still young and wasn't trying to be locked down. He was my main nigga, but I had to keep my options open, you know.

I checked my phone and noticed all the missed calls I had from Brazil. She's probably pissed Brittany let me stay over at Kimmy's last night. Along with those, I had a few texts from my homegirls, and one from an unknown number.

'Hey pretty can u get away tonight?' I skimmed over the message and started typing out a reply: *'Idk yet I stayed out last night, and you know how they are'*

Just as I was about to place my phone on the night stand it buzzed again. I turned on the screen to read, *'Yea I Know, well hit me up if u get away'*

I really had to get Zil to let me stay out tonight, I *had* to see UNKNOWN. It had been a while since we kicked it. I bet you're wondering who that is, huh? Well, I'll fill you in later on. I don't think you're ready to know about all my little linkups just yet.

Close your eyes, ain't no point in looking
Over here with the weak shit
Get out of here with the weak shit
You won't get nowhere with that

I had your type before,
No, I don't want that back
Don't want that back
You talk fiction, I talk facts

—Ella Mai

CHAPTER 3

Brazil

I was so mad Brittany let Bianca stay the night at Kimmy's. She knew her mama was out of town, and she knew Bianca was hot in the ass. I mean, come on, she just got caught kissing some random in Mrs. Laran's basement. I swear, the harder I try to keep Bebe out of trouble, the more she gets into it. Brittany was not as hard on her as I was.

She had too many of our mama's ways in her, and I knew one slip-up and she'd be going down the wrong path. Don't get me wrong, Brittany was hard on her too, but she also spoiled her with any and everything she wanted. Me, on the other hand, I made her work or earn anything she wanted. "Brittany, you heard from Bebe yet?" I screamed up the stairs to my sister.

"No, not yet. Have you called her, Zil?" she asked me, knowing I have called her over ten times at this point.

I exhaled through my nose. "It's two PM and she hasn't returned my calls or answered my texts. She was supposed to shampoo for me today at the shop," I said, walking in to my sister's room and flopping on her bed.

"I'm sure she's fine, Zil, it's summertime, let her live a little! I do think we have been a little hard on her, she *is* sixteen now," Brittany chided, sitting up and looking at me.

Rubbing the bridge of my nose, I rolled over onto my back so I could look up at her. "Yes, I know but she so wild," I sighed. "I don't want her to end up like Mama." I got up, walked in her bathroom, and called Bebe again. She still didn't answer, but I didn't have time for her today. I had two sew-ins to do at three thirty, so I need to get ready to go if I was going to make it to downtown Detroit in enough time.

I hopped out of the shower and walked into my room to throw something on. After getting dressed, I looked at myself in the mirror to assist me in pulling my long hair back out of my face. My dark skin glowed because of the coconut oil gel I just applied, but I could see the worry behind my eyes.

Ever since Mama left, I stressed myself out about how me and my sisters would survive. Yeah, Brittany's boyfriend Xavier took care of us for a while, Britt started dancing, and don't get me wrong, we were doing good, but I wanted more for myself than doing hood celebrities' hair every day.

I wanted to move away and be a writer; I wanted to travel the world, but I pushed those thoughts to the back of my mind, because although Britt took care of us, I was the one who held everything together.

I made sure the bills were paid, kept up with the taxes on the house—basically anything important, I handled it. Britt just gave me the money. Since I began doing hair fulltime, I helped too. Brittany loves clothes and jewelry, so after she paid her part of the bills, she was at that mall, keeping her and Bebe laced in the finest.

****

I was on my last frontal install. Since I clocked in, I had seven sew-ins and I was dog tired but I knew Ron would be there soon to meet me so we could hang out.

Ron was my boyfriend; we had been together since we were about fourteen. He wasn't no hood nigga at all, he was just *from* the hood. Ron went to school and worked at Home Depo after. He was what my sisters called lame, but hell, they called me lame, so I guess we here perfect for each other.

As I locked the shop up, I walked up to my car, and Ron was leaning up against the door. "Hey, Love," he greeted, grabbing my waist and pulling me in for a kiss.

"Do we really have to go out today? Can we just chill at the house? I'm tired..." I requested, even though I knew he was going to be mad the moment he heard the question. He was big on us doing the dating thing, but I just wasn't up for it tonight. Plus, I had an appointment early in the morning.

"Bae, you know how I feel 'bout goin' out and spending time together!" he pointed out with an attitude. "I'm 'bout to start school in a few weeks and pick up more hours at work, so we need to spend as much time together as we can."

"I know that, but I'm tired, Ron. I don't feel like it today."

I pulled away from him and hit the unlock button on my car. "Really, Zil? You just gon' blow me off knowing we haven't hung in a week?"

Dropping my head back and trying not to groan, I told him, “Ron, I know, but I’m tired and I don’t feel like all that today. I’ll call you later.” If I didn’t just walk away, we would be going back and forth all day. I hopped in my car, blew him a kiss, and pulled off.

If this was happening a few years ago, I would’ve just gone, because that’s how much I enjoyed being with Ron. These days, however, he had begun to irritate me. He was so *clingy;* I need some space sometimes. He still wanted to fall asleep on the phone, or he would want to text the whole day knowing I had hair to do my entire shift. I might be outgrowing him.

I pulled up to my house and saw about three cars out front, which immediately told me Brittany had company staying over. “Hey, Y’all,” I greeted as I walked through the door.

Brittany, Xavier, Xavier’s cousin Kwame, and two of Britt’s friends sat in the living room, smoking. Not too far into the kitchen was Bianca and her friend Kimmy. I wanted to cuss Bianca out for that bullshit she pulled, but I wasn’t about to go there with her.

As I walked upstairs to my room, I felt Kwame grab my arm and spin me around to look at him. “Kwame, Go on, I’m not in the mood!” I hissed at him

He just laughed. “Zil, you’re never in the mood, but one day, I’mma change that.” Then, he leaned in again.

In feigned disgust, I leaned back out of range, turning my face away. “Boy, go on. I’m not ‘bout to go there with u today!” I clapped back.

Kwame has been trying to get with me for years, and don't get me wrong, he was fine. Light skin with smoke grey eyes, nice, pink, juicy lips. His dreads were even pulled up in a ponytail, and he always smelled so good, but he was a hood nigga, and I didn't do those. Plus, I was with Ron, and I was a virgin. All niggas like him wanted to do was fuck.

He pulled me close to him, close enough that our lips almost touched. "Stop playing, Zil, and let me take you out," he whispered. I opened my mouth to say something, but no words came out. I was feeling hot all overlooking into his light eyes—I went into a trance.

The sound of my phone snapped me out of it. "Bye, Kwame, you know I got a man," I mumbled as I pulled away and walked upstairs to my room.

Ron was blowing my phone up, which irritated me more with him than I already was. Like, I haven't been home but thirty minutes, and he was already calling and texting, asking why I haven't called him yet. He made me so mad sometimes, but he was the only guy I had ever been with. I was used to him, but maybe it was time for a change.

Something in the walls,
Something in your walk looks different.
Something deep inside
Got me wondering why I don't understand.
Why I can't put my finger on what the fuck is up.
What's missing?

You distant, and I'm spinning.
Don't ask questions usually
Got the answers that I need.
Intuition telling me...

—Ella Mai

CHAPTER 4

Me and Zay had been on good terms lately. He even postponed his little trip because I was mad at him for ditching me the other day. We all sat in the living room, drinking and smoking. Just vibing. 42 Duggs' *The Street* played on the sound bar when I got up to go get another bottle of D'Ussé off the bar.

"Damn, Britt. When Zil gon' stop playin'?" Kwame asked as he pulled from the blunt Zay just passed him.

I laughed. "Boy, please. You know my sister ain't fucking with you."

"Watch, one day I'mma get her, you'll see." He shrugged at me, and I rolled my eyes, amused by his insistence. "I'll change her life."

Kwame was crazy, there wasn't no way that Zil would give him a change with how she was so hooked on Ron's lame ass. But hey, if that's what she likes.

We took a few shots and smoked like three more blunts. As I put the last blunt out, I heard a bang on the door. "Who is it?" I yelled. It was about twelve AM, who could be knocking *this* late?

I didn't get a response, so I yelled "Who the FUCK is it?!" again as I walked to the door. Now Kwame and Zay were behind me with their guns pulled.

"Zay, I know you over here, I tracked your phone!" a woman's voice spoke out. I knew right then that it was Zay's baby mama Krystal.

Zay pushed me to the side and opened the door. "What the fuck, bitch?!"

She butted up into him, trying to make him take a step back. "Boy, cut it out! You know I was gon' come looking for you with your lying ass!" she screeched as she pointed her finger in his face.

I stepped in between them. "Look, hoe, you done lost your whole mind thinking you 'bout to come over here with that bullshit!" I said while pulling my long, bone straight hair in a ponytail.

"Bitch, this ain't even for you," Krystal scoffed, but she was backpedaling. She was pretty as hell, but man, she was the biggest hoe in the hood. She had fucked and sucked every nigga around the block.

Undeterred, I marched forward. "I don't care who it's for, but you better get the fuck on before I beat that ass again!" Her eyes were as wide as dinner plates.

Zay pulled me back. "Yo, y'all chill out!" Then, he took over for me. "Krystal, get the fuck on with your weak ass, always on some bullshit!"

Her face was red. She opened her mouth a few times and closed it again, before finally snapping, "Boy, stop lyin' so much! You said you was goin' OT but made a mistake and pocket dialed me. I been listening to you and your li'l stripper bitch laugh all night!"

"Bitch, keep talking crazy about my sister an' I'mma pop you in the mouth," I hear Zil say from behind me. See,

Brazil was the quite stuck up one, but when she got mad or when someone was fucking with her family, she would pop off and act a complete fool. She was like our daddy.

I held a hand up. “Zil, I got this.” I stared down Krystal. “Listen, bitch, how many times do I have to tell you? Nothin’ you can do or say will stop Zay from fucking with me. You just his BM, your name don’t hold no weight.”

“BITCH—” and all I heard was a loud smack. Zil had slapped the shit out of Krystal as soon as the word ‘bitch’ left her mouth. Before I knew it, her and Bebe were beating the shit out of her.

Kwame pulled Zil off her, and I grabbed Bebe. Zay finished the procession by cussing Krystal out as he picked her up off the ground and pushed her down the porch to her car.

I couldn’t believe this shit. Here it is, every time we were on good terms, some bullshit happened. I had a feeling something would go down. Every time me and Zay are in a good space, some bullshit pops off. I’m tired of it. Really, it was always something with him and that rat-ass baby mama he got.

This wasn’t the first time Krystal and me had a problem; it was normal. She was bitter as fuck, but in a way, she wasn’t wrong. I mean, Zay was playing both sides. I knew he was a cheater. I knew he was a liar. I am the only one blinded by it, and the only one who continues to fuck with him. I knew he wasn’t right, but he held me down when no one else was there. He took care of my little sisters.

I know it might sound dumb, but I felt like I owed him loyalty. Zil always said, “Britt, you didn’t ask him for nothin', he did it on his own. You shouldn't let him disrespect you like that." Her words echoed through my mind even now.

I watch Zay talk to Krystal from the porch. I hated that he was even holding a conversation with her after she came over disrespecting me and my home. I deserve better, but hey, I knew that. But would I really leave him alone? Could I really part ways with someone who had my back at my darkest times?

I hate feeling like this. I was the strong one out of all of us, I never showed emotion about anything. I never let my sisters see me stress, I always played the 'everything is going to be okay!' role. Holding us down and holding all my emotions in was starting to wear me out. I needed a break.

But how could I say I needed a break when I had so much, I was responsible for? I could never leave my sisters hanging. Yeah, Brazil took care of all the important stuff, but I was the *glue*. I couldn't take a break until I knew my sisters were going to be straight.

We ain't even been talking for a minute yet

And I already got you elevated.

You don't know if I'mma saint or a sinner yet

But you already singing Ella praises

—Ella Mai

CHAPTER 5

BRAZIL

I can't believe this bitch Krystal has the nerve to come over here playing crazy with my sister. I beat her ass, so Brittany didn't have to. I was sick of watching her go through that mess with Zay. I wish she would leave his no-good ass alone. But Brittney was grown. You couldn't tell her nothin'.

I seem to be the only one with some sense. My little sister was a *hoe.* She swore she was being sneaky, but we all knew Bianca was a slut. She didn't hide it very well. Every time a group of niggas was around, Bianca was right in the middle of them.

Brittany was dick dizzy, every time Zay fucked her, she forgot about all the bullshit he did and was right up under him, riding his coat tail. They were so embarrassing sometimes, but they were my sisters, and nobody better ever disrespect them or it's over. I may seem like I'm quiet and I honestly don't like drama, but I'm diehard about them; they're all I got, so yes, of course I whooped Krystal's ass with no problem.

I knew Brittany was going to cuss Zay out not answering his calls for about a week, and then before I know it, he'll be right back over her. She's so dumb, I would never deal with that. I'm sure you think I'm on a high horse, but I'm not. I just want what's best for my sisters, you know?

By the way, I have a little tea to tell, too. I may be with Ron, but I'm really starting to like Kwame. I don't know why, but I just do. I know he's bad for me, and I know all he wants is sex, but when I saw him tonight, I got chills. Everybody thought I was hooked on Ron, but he had started to get on my nerves. I was ready for something new, but I knew Kwame wasn't it.

I walked past my sister as she sat there and listened to Zay feed her lies about Krystal, disappearing into the kitchen to fix me something to eat. I was tired and was ready to chill. As I looked through the fridge to get out the stuff for my chicken salad, I closed the door and there was Kwame standing there, staring into my eyes with his sexy ass.

I couldn't let him *know* I thought he was sexy though, so I put that wall up. "Damn, Kwame. You don't got nowhere else to be than creeping around my kitchen?"

"I do, but Zay ain't ready, so I'm here."

I rolled my eyes and continued to make my salad "You want some?" I asked Kwame. He was just standing there watching me and being a creep, so I decided to stop being mean, since I knew he wasn't going to leave me alone

He reanimated, moving off the wall instead of staring me down like I was an animal on a nature documentary. "Yeah, sure. I was waiting to see if you were gon' keep being rude."

"How is it rude when I told you to leave me alone hours ago, you the one who don't get it. I told you, I got a man.

Kwame was laughing so hard at me telling him I had a man. I didn't find it so humorous. "What's funny?"

"You funny. You keep saying you got a man, but every time I look at you, you can't make eye Contact and you squeeze your thighs together," he pointed out as he walked closer and closer to me.

I couldn't help but blush on my way to push past him and walk to my room. He was right. I had to get away from him, my panties were melting, and I knew that was wrong. I love Ron. Kwame followed me to my room, and as soon as I tried to close the door, he stopped me with his hand. "Why you so mean all the time, Zil?" he inquired.

My eyes went wide. "I'm not. I just don't entertain others while I'm in a relationship," I replied coyly.

"You've been in relationship with ol' boy since forever, so when have you ever had the chance to entertain?" he asked.

"Kwame, go on, I need to study. I don't have time to play these games with you," I snorted while sitting on my bed and pulling my laptop out. I had taken two classes this summer, and I had finals in a week and two five-thousand-word papers due.

He grinned wide. "Zil, let me help you study, then," he said as he sat down next to me, and the smell of Jimmy Cho mixed with weed filled my nostrils.

I felt butterflies in my stomach the closer he moved next to me. "Okay, fine, 'cause I know you're goin' to keep bugging me," I muttered, rolling my eyes. Deep down though, I really didn't want him to leave.

"Cool, what you want me to do?"

Even though he had already called me on it earlier, I avoided eye contact when he spoke. "Ask me the question I have wrote on the flashcards and I'll answer them." I handed him the cards I had one of my classmates make for me, and we got to work

Two hours had passed, and I was finishing up. "Damn, girl. You smart as hell, you got all the questions right," Kwame exclaimed as he laid the cards down on the bed.

Bowing my head at the compliment, I suppressed a smile. "I worked so hard to pass this class, hopefully I don't freeze up when it's time to take my final." I stood up and stretched my legs, a yawn gliding out before I could muffle it back. "Okay, well thanks for your help, Kwame. I'm getting ready to shower and go to bed, I have a class early," I explained, hinting for his departure as I grabbed my robe off my chair in the corner.

Kwame stood up and walked up close to me—so close I could smell the double mint gum on his breath. As soon as he wrapped his arms around me to give me a hug, I melted a little on the inside, laid my head in the middle of his chest, took deep breath, and inhaled his scent.

I jumped back as soon as I begin to get lost in his touch. "Bye, Kwame!" I blurted as I walked out the room and hurried to the bathroom. What was going on with me? I'm with Ron! I couldn't believe Kwame was making me feel like this—I have *never* felt like this before.

As I undressed, I could still smell him on my hoodie. I held the pullover up to my nose and took it all in. Before I knew it, I was wet just off his scent. Ignoring the feeling, I stepped into the shower and let the hot water down my body, dropping my head back so I could feel the piping steam open my pores. Blindly, I grabbed my rose water and pink sea salt body scrub, lathered up my loofa, and began washing up. When I got to my pussy, I found myself getting hot, and Kwame's face popped in my head.

It wasn't something I was proud of, but I inserted two of my freshly manicured fingers into my opening. With a whimper, I moved them in and out while fantasizing about Kwame's golden skin, naked in the shower, with me playing with my clit. I leaned up against the wall and placed my leg up on the side of the tub.

In my mind, his lips where soft as he kissed on my neck, his rough hands felt so good as he rubbed my nipples. I moaned his name loudly as I came all over my fingers. Even *after* getting off, I continued to pleasure myself as I thought about having sex with Kwame. I was in a trance, cumming back-to-back while screaming his name

BOOM, BOOM.

There was a knock at the door that snatched me back to reality. "Y... Yeah, I'm in here!" I yelled to whoever was knocking.

"I know you were calling my name."

My heart jumped into my throat. Oh my God, did he hear me? "No, I didn't—!" I was so *embarrassed.* Did he know what I was doing? I wonder who else heard me...

His tongue clicked. "Yes, you did. I was on my way downstairs and I heard you yell 'KAWAME!'" When he mocked me, I felt like a boiled lobster, sitting in the steamy shower with a red face.

I had to think quick. What was I going to say? *I had to think quick.* "Um—oh! Yeah, can you hand me a new towel from the linen closet?" I lied as I turned the water off. Pulling back the curtain, I cracked the door and stuck my hand out to grab the towel.

"Yeah, Zil, I'll grab it," he assured. Now I was left standing there, shivering and naked, waiting for him to get back. Soon the knob turned, but to my surprise, he pushed into the bathroom. I jumped back, grabbing the towel from him fast and covering my naked body. "Don't cover up now, I know you wasn't screaming my name for no towel," he teased, laughing, but looking into my eyes.

"Yes, I was." I was trying not to blush. "Now Bye, Kwame."

He pulled back, exhaling through his nose. "Yeah, okay, Zil. The way you was calling my name, you would've thought… You know what, never mind. I'm UP." I pushed the door closed behind him and dropped myself against it. Oh my God, what am I doing? Was it crazy that I was now mad he left after I was the one who told him to leave? I can't believe I'm tripping like this.

You don't need to call anymore

Don't fuck with you at all anymore

You don't need to stall anymore

Anymore

—Ella Mai

CHAPTER 6

BIANCA

Staring at the GLOW Period Tracker app on my phone, I slowly came to terms with the fact that I was two weeks late for my period. My jaw was on the floor. I had to find out if I was pregnant—and fast—so I could take care of that problem. I don't care how fast I act or how grown I try to be, I wasn't ready for no baby.

With my head spinning, I called my best friend Carlos, he was the only person I could trust. "Best-friend!" I yelled the moment the phone stopped ringing.

"What's up, Bebe?"

Flattening my lips, I couldn't find the words to speak for a good minute. They flew out of me: "I need you to go to CVS and get me a pregnancy test!" Once I was finished, I cringed, already knowing the response I'd get.

He proved it was for good reason when he started groaning. "Man, Bebe, for real? You tripping, man. So you just out here letting—"

I cut him off in mid-sentence. "Listen, I don't need that right now. I'm scared as hell, are you gon' go do it or not?"

Carlos sighed. "Yeah, man, I'll be over in a little bit."

****

The two pink lines stood out bright as *hell.* I couldn't believe I was pregnant. I cried for at least three hours in my room. What was I going to do? I had to get an abortion before my nosy as sisters find out. They would kill me and would never let me get rid of the baby.

I had to figure out how I was going to get the money and get everything taken care of—and fast. I knew who's baby it was, I was just scared to tell him. This couldn't be happening to me. But I guess God don't like ugly. I decided to send him a text and let him know what was up. *'Hey 911 can u please call me it's important'*

There I sat, waiting for a response while trying not to grind my teeth. That failed when my phone finally buzzed, and his text came in. *'Man, Bebe I can't call right now what's up'*

This is what I hated about him. I made myself available to him whenever, but as soon as I called or needed him, he was busy. *'IM PREGNANT !!!! I WASNT GON TEXT IT BUT SINCE YOU SO BUSY .... I don't know what u want to do but I don't want it!'*

He texted quickly this time. *'HOW MUCH YOU NEED'*

I didn't even text back. He really was an asshole. I mean, even though I wanted an abortion in the first place, he could have at least asked me if I was sure or offered to talk about it! But all he did was ask how much. How much?

I should keep his money and this baby, that would show him. It would blow up his whole little world. Then we'll see if he's busy. I was so mad I was thinking crazy; I knew I couldn't keep this baby, but he didn't know that. I had a plan.

Bet you're wondering who he is. It's not Marcus. I wish it was, then I might consider keeping it...

My phone dinged at a new text alert. *'????? How much so u can make your appointment?'* I left him on read. Who does he think he is, acting like my baby didn't matter? I don't want the baby and that was a fact, but the more he acted like he didn't care about me the more I was changing my mind.

The least he could do was ask me how I felt, and he couldn't even do that. As everything set in, I could feel my rage boiling—I was pissed.

Suddenly, a thought hit me. I knew how I was going to pay for it. I'd have Carlos loan me the money and block this nigga. He would never know if I went or not—he would be on pins and needles for months.

I was sick of him acting like he was so high and mighty. I'd show his ass. But first, I had to figure out how I would get the money for my abortion without asking my sisters. I couldn't believe my life right now. I really wished I could call my mom in that moment. I knew my sisters didn't fuck with Mama, but I still loved her, and even more, I planned on reaching out to her. I needed her.

I'd try to find her; it couldn't be too hard. She would call Brittany sometimes, threatening to come get me if Brittany and Brazil wouldn't give her money. I had to tell someone—I couldn't do this alone. Carlos was probably clueless to what was going on my head, wondering what the test said.

I'm so lost right now; this can't be life. "Man, Bebe, what you going to do with a baby?" Carlos asked.

Blinking, I just sat there looking crazy. "I'm not having no baby, Los," I mechanically responded. "I got shit to do and a baby will slow me down, like, for real." At this point, my eyes were already lasered onto my phone. I was on Google searching up my mama. I knew that I'd need her to get the abortion, because although she left me with Zil and Britt, she never gave them guardianship over me.

I was going to need her to sign for me to get it. Then, I'd have to figure out how I was going to get her to do it without telling my sisters. I might have to pay her, but where would I get the money from? I already had to get abortion money, and I know she going to want at least five hundred bucks to keep her mouth shut.

"So, you gonna tell Marcus?"

His question took me away from my train of thought. *"No*—and you not either, don't open your mouth to *nobody*. Not even Kimmy!" I firmly instructed.

I watched Carlos' eyebrows shoot up. "What you mean no?! You have to tell him," he argued, folding his arms in disapproval. "It's only right."

He was on some Bro Code bullshit, and now it was my turn to groan. "No, I don't. It's not his business, Los. Chill, man, I got this. Just let me think, please' The last part was muttered as I continued to scroll my phone.

Carlos wasn't giving up that easily. He doubled down, staring me in the face even though I was obviously trying not to look at him. "Man, Bebe," he huffed. "You tripping, that's that man's baby and you just gon' kill it and not say nothin' to him about it. You wrong as hell. He might want you to keep it, you never know, Bebe."

I wasn't trying to hear a thing he was saying. He was getting on my nerves already, and I only knew I was pregnant for four hours at that point. I had to hurry and find my mama before Los went and started running his mouth to Marcus. I couldn't have that. Instead, I'd make it my business to find my mama, but I had to hurry, because this could all go bad before I knew it.

Don't know what I'm capable of

Might fuck around and go crazy on Cuz.

Might fuck around, have to pay me in blood

—Jhene Aiko

CHAPTER 7

♥*BRITTANY*♥

I had been off Zay for about a week now. I listened to his lies after my sisters fought Krystal, but I really was sick of him. I know he was there for me when I need it the most, but I swear, I didn't deserve to be treated like that. I was ready for something new.

I would have to move away to find someone though, because Zay was everybody in Detroit's plug. Niggas were scared to even look my way. He had told them I was off-limits. I only made money at work because niggas felt like they were kissing his ass by "making it rain on Zay's girl."

That shit was crazy to me. You would think it would be disrespectful to throw money at your boss' girl. These niggas were so dick-sucked out they would do anything to get noticed by Zay.

I was in the dressing room at work getting changed into my last outfit for the night, buzzing and ready to get my stage show over with. Every week I did a stage show with this other dancer Passion. We always made ten thousand or better apiece. We had niggas from all over come see our show.

Tonight, it was a full house, and I was ready to put on a show. "Lovely and Passion, y'all up next!" the house mother yelled.

I stood in the mirror and made sure everything was in place. I had on a diamond studded G-string, and my ass was sitting perfect in the white fishnet boy shorts I had over it, just like how my breasts sat perched up in a diamond-studded halter top. I had my real hair flat ironed bone-straight with a part down the middle, and to complete it all, I sprayed some Bath and Body Works shimmer body oil over my creamy brown skin. I was ready to perform.

"Coming to the stage for tonight's stage show, what all y'all niggas be waiting on: Lovely and Passion!"

Jhene Aiko's *Pussy Fairy* played loud throughout the club. I walked to the pole and started dancing, winding my hips slowly to the beat. As soon as I began climbing the pole, Passion was at the bottom, dancing slowly to the music.

"'Cause I got you sprung off in the springtime
Fuck all your free time
You don't need no me time
That's you and me time.
We be getting so loud
That dick makes my soul smile"

The beat dropped, and when it did, I slid down and busted the splits on top of Passion's face, which I rode like she was giving me head. The crowd was going crazy, and the stage was *covered* in money. We pushed it to the side and continued the show.

The two of us danced on each other like we were fucking to the music. Towards the end of our final song, Passion bent over and made her ass clap while I did some pole tricks. I glided down, bent over, and kissed her on the mouth. As soon as I did, they were throwing so much money I couldn't see the crowd anymore.

The night was finally winding down. "We made a little over fifteen thousand bucks tonight," I noted to Passion as I counted and separated our money.

After every show, we would bag up our money and take it back to Passion's house and count it. Currently, I was in between her legs, laying back in her lap. "I figured we did, they was in there deep as fuck tonight," she said from behind me on the floor.

Suddenly, Passion pulled my head back and kissed me as she slipped her hands down my biker shorts, rubbing my throbbing clit with her fingers. I spin around so now we were facing each other, she pulled my sports bra over my head, and my perfect full breasts fell out. They sat up just as they would if I had a bra on.

She pulled away from our kiss and placed her warm mouth on my chocolate-chip-colored nipple. As she sucked on the buds, I put my hands under her T-shirt, and I knew she didn't have on any underwear—I felt her bald pussy dripping. Grinning, I slipped two fingers inside and her warm juices ran down my hand.

Passion was so gentle with me, I think that's why I liked her. When I was fucking with Zay, he was so rough all the time. Passion explored my body and she kissed me everywhere a girl wanted to be kissed.

With Passion, things weren't complicated. Well, not between us it wasn't. When we were together, it was like a breath of fresh air. Besides, on top of our little fling we had going on, we also made money together. I knew this couldn't last forever, but in the meantime, I was gonna enjoy the feeling of her warm tongue dancing with mine.

Think it's best

I put my heart on ice (heart on ice)

Cause I can't breathe

I'mma put my heart on ice (heart on ice)

It's getting the best of me

—Rod Wave

CHAPTER 8

Xavier

I had been calling Brittany for three hours and still wasn't getting an answer. She really knew how to piss me off. I know you think I'm a bad guy, but I'm not. Let me introduce myself. I'm Xavier Maxwell—Or Zay.

I run Detroit and a few cities in Indiana, Ohio, and New York, and I've been in the game since I was fifteen years old. My pops died when I was eleven, and I had to help my mama take care of my two little sisters.

I started by standing at the gas station selling dime bags. One day, a big Mexican looking dude rode up and told me he had been watching me work for about a year and asked if I wanted to make more money working for him. I told him sure, why not. I needed the money to help Mama out. I haven't looked back since.

Beto showed me how to sell every drug around. He was the plug, and he took me under his wing. He was like a father to me, he even showed me the route in Mexico. He was the one that introduced me to a lot of people that looked out for me since I had gotten in the game. Beto made me to promise to keep things going if anything was to happen to him, and I made kept that promise.

About two years ago, Beto died from cancer, and he left me in charge of the East Coast states. His son Javier was in charge of the West Coast states. Unfortunately, me and Javier didn't really get along so well.

He always felt like I was taking his dad from him, because Beto looked out for me when I had nothing. I owed him everything, so Javier felt like he cared for me more, but that wasn't true.

Regardless of how his son felt, I listened to Beto. I took everything said and taught to me very seriously and used it all to become who I was today. The King of Detroit. I had my own team, now. I was in charge, using everything Beto taught me to run my empire and I worked hard to get where I was. I had drug houses running on at least three blocks on every side of town. Beto trusted me with the business, so I had to keep everything up and running.

I moved my mama and sisters out to Florida about three years ago. She was set up real nice. I even paid for my sisters to go to the best private schools in the state. Every year, I put a hundred racks in a savings account for them. When they turned eighteen, I was going to give it to them so no matter what they decided to do, they would be set for life.

I made sure they didn't need for anything in the world—they would never go through what I went through. Nights with no food, days with no hot water or heat. When all this was going on, my sister Lisa was still a baby and Mama didn't have Lashay yet.

She came years later, when Mama had met a guy. Me and him didn't get along. He said I thought I was grown. I mean, in age I wasn't, but in my mind, I was. After all, I took care of everything around the house. I paid the bills and put food on the table.

Mama worked at a diner and brought home money, but not enough to take care of things. When Jake moved in, a lot changed. Mama stopped letting me pay the bills and let Jake handle everything. Me and him bumped heads more than anything, and I found myself staying away more and more.

One day I came to Mama's house just to check in, and there was an eviction letter taped to the door. Not only that, but the mailbox was full of past-due bills. I didn't understand. Mama fought with me to get me to stop taking care of things and let Jake do it and look what was happening.

Confused and looking for answers, I opened the door, and my mama was passed out on the floor alone—my little sister Lisa was nowhere to be found.

I called 911.

Hours later, I was finally able to talk to my mama and check on her. "Hey, Mama. You good?" I asked as I walked into her hospital room.

The warm smile she gave me had my chest panging with relief. "Yes, Baby, I'm fine and feeling better," she assured. "I don't know what happened! One minute I was walking to the back room to put the clothes away, then the next thing I know, I'm being woke up by doctors."

She fell silent, but I could tell there was more she wanted to say, so I didn't respond to the story much. "The doctor said I'd be fine, I was just dehydrated, and... I'm pregnant, Zay-Zay"

"What, Mama? Aww man, how are you going to take care of another baby? I seen the eviction notice, I seen all the bills past due, Mama," I pointed out to her.

Tears quickly filled her eyes. "Jake left me, Zay. I been trying to make ends meet, but I can't do it alone." Her head hung low. "I didn't want to call you because I pushed you away before," she mumbled while crying softly.

This was insane. "No matter what happened in the past, I will always be there for you and my sister no matter what!" I yelled. I couldn't believe she let it get this bad. "Where is Lisa?" I asked, worried. I didn't need no more time bad news.

"Oh, she's with her friend for the weekend..."

At least that was one thing I wouldn't have to take care of tonight. "Good," I muttered. "Mama, I'm going to go to your house and clean up. I'll take care of the bills, but you have to promise me some stuff: you will never let a man come between us, ever. Secondly, you will never call Jake and speak of this baby. I'll help you take care of it."

It took a while for her to answer. I knew this would be hard for her. Since my daddy died, Mama let men control her; she let them come in and turn her world upside down. I was always there to pick up the pieces, but when Jake came around, she wouldn't let me fix it. She believed he would be there for her and Lisa, but he wasn't.

To my relief, she put on a smile. "Okay, Zay. I promise."

Ring, Ring! My phone sounding off grabbed me from my thoughts. "Yeah, Krystal? What's up?" It came off a lot more sideways than I meant it to, but I didn't fix my tone. Thinking about Jake got my blood boiling, and she wouldn't make it any better.

"Umm..." She tentatively began. "What you doing, Zay?" Before I could answer, she added "I'm sorry about the other day. I won't do it again..."

"Krystal, I don't have time for your games!"

She gulped, silent. "I'm not playing, I'm sorry!" I heard her squeak when she eventually mustered up the courage to speak again. "I know you love Brittany, I know you want to be with her, but you never gave us a chance! You never let me show you I could be as good to you as she is."

My free hand rubbed at my temple, and I quickly tuned her out. "Man, I'm not trying to hear all that today, Krystal. Where's my daughter at?"

"Demi is with my mama, so why not come over here so we can talk?" I didn't have time for Krystal's games. I really wanted things to work with Brittany, but every time I try to do right, she be on some bullshit.

Like now, for instance, I had been calling her all night, and she wasn't answering. We were just cool the other day. I mean, yeah, I had been gone for two days, but she knew when I was on business, I usually turned my personal phone off. I don't need any distractions when dealing with that shit.

Brittany felt like I should at least send her a text every now and then to let her know I was okay. She felt like I owed her that much, anyway. She wanted me to let her in my world, and I didn't think I should. What I did had nothing to do with her, and I wanted to keep it that way.

Krystal didn't let me think about it for too long. *"Zay!* Are you coming?"

"Yes, I'm on my way."

Dreaming (I might be)

Man, I must be dreaming.

Dreaming, dreaming

Dreaming (I might Be)

—Young Jeezy

CHAPTER 9

Bianca

It had been three weeks and I still haven't found my mama, which meant I was eight weeks pregnant now. I didn't want to ask Brittany how to find her, but I had no choice. The only thing was, I had to have a reason that I wanted to talk to her.

Brittany and Brazil did everything they could to make sure I didn't miss Mama. I never really did. I mean, when I was young, I cried about missing her, or when I got caught doing something I knew I had no business doing I used missing mama as an excuse of why I did it. In reality, though, I had made peace with the whole thing.

I really didn't care about her leaving us anymore. I felt like it was what it was. If she loved us like real mothers loved their kids, then she would still be here, not nowhere to be found. I was just going have to ask about her.

I walked in the living room where Brittany and Brazil were sitting, and I sat down next to Zil. "So, I been thinking about mama a lot lately..." I started to explain to my sisters. "Before y'all get mad, just hear me out:

I miss Mama. Y'all got so many more years with her then I did, I was little when she left. I didn't even get to know her!" Even though I was just saying all of this to get the excuse to talk to her and get her help, it made my throat close up. "I really wish y'all would just let me talk to her. I know what she did, and I know how y'all feel about it, and I promise not to get to in my feelings 'bout it, I promise!" I blurted out before they could say anything.

Brittany was frowning before I was even finished giving my speech. "Bebe, don't start that shit," she snapped. "If Mama wanted to get to know you or wanted you to know her, she wouldn't have left you with us, she would've taken you with her!"

Her voice had jumped to a yell at this point, and I couldn't help but to match her tone. "So, you still mad about that, Britt?!" I snarled. "It was years ago, she might have changed!"

"If she changed, then she'd be back here with us. *We ain't went nowhere!"* She was screaming now. "We in the same spot we was when she left!"

The whole time, Zil was quiet. She continued to read her book, not saying a word. She didn't even look up. "Zil, what you think?" I asked anxiously.

The only sound that filled the room was the dry turn of a page, paper brushing over paper. "I think you should do whatever you want Bianca," Zil said while still not looking up from her book.

"Are you serious right now?" Brittany shouted.

"Very." Brazil responded, still not looking up.

That was the last thing our older sister wanted to hear at this point, I fell quiet. "I can't believe you think it's okay for her to reach out to her after all she put us through—after how hard we worked to keep everything together without her." Brittany shook her head as she stood up to walk away.

Brazil exhaled. "I'm *just saying,* if she wants to talk to her, let her talk. She'll see in the end," she simply stated and continued to read.

I knew this would make my sisters fight, and I knew how they both felt about Mama—truth be told, I really didn't want to get to know her, I just need to get this abortion before I got too far along.

Before I could say anything else, Brittany handed me a piece of paper she was writing on. "Here is all her information. When she hurt your little feelings, don't come crying to me, 'cause she will." Without another word, she walked upstairs.

I knew Britt was mad because she tried her best to take care of me. She might be feeling that because I asked about Mama, I didn't appreciate her, but I'm doing all of this for a reason. Soon it would be all over, and I'd put this behind me.

I dialed the number on the paper, fingers shaky. "Hello?"

"Mama, it's me, Bebe."

And I don't know why I'm even still here

Can't shake it off, I've been here for years on top of years

And I'm ready to—I'm ready to be off you

Cause I admit that, Baby, I might be stuck on you

—Kehlani

CHAPTER 10

Brazil

I was curling my last client for the day. The fourth of July was tomorrow, and I had been working all day. I wasn't complaining though, because the money was good. What was complaint worthy was the fact that Ron had been blowing my phone up for the last couple days. I felt bad that I was giving him the cold shoulder, but I just wasn't feeling Ron anymore. We had grown apart.

I finally answered his call. "Yes, Ron?"

"So you don't see me calling you, Zil?!" he yelled.

Miraculously, my sympathy evaporated. "Yeah, Ron. I'm working, and you know that. I texted you this morning and told you that I had a busy day today," I quipped in response.

It was a good thing I had pulled my face away from the phone the first time he hollered, because he was keeping it going now. "Yeah, you did, but I texted and asked could I take you to lunch you never answered me, Zil."

"I was working, Ronald, I can't keep my phone in my hand and do hair at the same time." I was starting to get irritated with Ron. He was changing, and I didn't like the new him.

Maybe he read my mind, because instead of doubling down with his complaints, he just sighed. "Zil, I just love you so much, and I'm ready to take this to the next level. We been together for so long—" Ron proceeded to drone on and on about something I didn't want to hear.

I think that was one reason why I wasn't feeling him anymore. He was trying to force me to have sex with him, and I wasn't ready. Yeah, I masturbated from time to time, but I couldn't go that far, and the more Ron pushed me, the more I didn't want to do it.

"Can we have dinner tonight, Zil?"

"Sure, Ron. I'll be over tonight after work."

Although I haven't really been feeling Ron lately, he was still my man, and I had been curving him a lot—I could at least sit down and have dinner with him. After all, we used to spend every minute of free time we had together. We had grown apart, but I still loved him. "Okay, Baby. See you soon!" Ron gushed.

Dinner had gone well, and I was surprised. Ron and I were enjoying ourselves; he had gone all out. Since Ron had his own small one-bedroom apartment in a little city outside of Detroit called Melvindale, he had lit candles all around the house and cooked my favorite meal: fried salmon, rice, and asparagus. Ron was in school to be a chef, plus his grandma taught him how to cook before she passed away.

We ate dinner and were now watching a movie on the Firestick while munching on ice cream; it kind of felt like old times. No fighting or fussing, just vibing like old times.

"Hey, you staying the night? If so, I will run your bath for you," Ron offered.

My shoulders lifted and then dropped in a shrug. "Yeah, sure, I guess. I don't have any clients 'til late tomorrow."

He grinned. "Great, just let me know when you're ready and I'll run your water," Ron instructed as he pulled me closer and went back to watching the TV.

After my bath, I went into the bedroom to dry off and lotion up. Just as promised, Ron had all my clothes spread out on the bed. He was really laying it on thick tonight. I didn't mind though, because I was enjoying it. Not one time did he annoy me.

I know you might be thinking that Ron sounds like a good guy and the only bad thing I could say about him is that he started being too clingy. No, there was a lot more to it than that.

A year ago, Ron cheated on me with a girl from school; we broke up. About a month after it, his grandma passed, and I couldn't let him go through that alone. I was there with him the whole time, and we kind of had been back together ever since.

Sadly, since then, he's been controlling and, on my heels, everywhere I go. I don't know if he thinks I'd cheat on him because he did it to me, kind of like a tit-for-tat kind of thing, but it wasn't like that; I really forgave him for what he did to me.

But, no matter how many times I told him that, I think deep down, he didn't believe that I was really over it. His problem was that he didn't forgive himself, and if he didn't forgive himself, then of course he didn't think I forgave him.

I rubbed coconut oil all over my creamy brown skin, slipped on the gray and black flannel, my black biker shorts, and a pair of pink fuzzy socks. Warm and ready for bed, I pulled my long, curly hair into a ponytail, and then I climbed into Ron's queen-size bed.

I needed to finish my journal entry for my class and place an order for some bundles for the hairline I was dropping on my birthday in a few weeks. I got comfortable and grabbed Ron's Apple iPad off the nightstand. I entered his password, and the tablet unlocked.

I logged in to my school classroom portal and completed my assignment, emailed my vendor, and placed an order for my hair. I was on the Gucci website looking for a new purse for Bianca's birthday, since it was the day after mine. As I scrolled the website, a message popped up from Facebook messenger. I ignored it and continued to do what I was doing.

Ping-ping. Ping!

It went off again. Something told me to look, but then again, I wasn't the snooping type; I never went looking for information, I let it find me. When I found out Ron was cheating, it wasn't because I went looking. Instead, the girl wrote me on Instagram. She told me everything.

Ping, ping!

I closed out of the Gucci site and there was his messenger, wide open. The first message was from 'The Real Alexis Carr.' It said, *'Damn so you acting funny tonight?'* There was another one, from Erica 'Love Myself' Wright: *'I had fun the other night'*

Now I was mad, so I decided to look at all of their message thread. I was so threw off by some of the stuff I was reading. Ron was on my coattail so hard because, for the last three months, he had been cheating on me. Pressing me to have sex with him, when the whole time, he was fucking maybe three different girls behind my back . I couldn't believe it.

Now, don't get me wrong, I don't put nothing past *nobody*. When you saw Ron and had a conversation with him, he was a well-rounded guy. Standing 6'2", very slim, and handsome. He had brown skin the same color as mine, and he wore his hair in a short cut.

Most importantly, he came from a two-parent household. Spoiled was an under-statement, he was the baby of four kids, and he had everything he every could think of. His apartment and car note were even paid for by his parents.

He always treated me so good. I thought he only cheated on me one time, but I guess this was his thing. Now, I know y'all are wondering how could I be mad, when I was just masturbating to the thought of Kwame?

I never really did anything with him, though. It was a dream, while Ron was taking girls out and fucking them. As much as I said he was getting on my nerves, I still loved him, and I had enjoyed him today, so my feelings were hurt. In fact, I was hurt more this time then the first time, because I talked all that forgiveness bullshit and now look what happened?

I continued to read through the messages. Not only was he cheating on me, but he was also lying and acting like I was some nagging-ass bitch that was always doing too much. When, in all reality, it was the other way around. He really was playing it crazy to them hoes. I was about to write them back from his page, but I just changed my mind.

I started putting my clothes on—I had to get out of there. I couldn't take it anymore; I was about to break down. My mind was all over the place. Ron was in the shower, so at least I could just leave and never look back. I left his iPad open so he would know it was over.

My heart was broke. Ron was my first love. I wanted to cry, but I couldn't find the strength to, as bad as I wanted to. I had sharp pain in my chest, and my head was spinning as I hurried to my car. I jumped in and pulled out my phone so I could block Ron on everything. I deleted our text thread, put my phone on DND, threw it in my purse, and drove away.

Okay, green light

Pistol in the party don't seem right.

Li'l bro off that molly, can't think right

It's about to be a fucking green light

—Rod Wave

CHAPTER 11

Kwame

Brazil had called my phone last night at two AM. I missed the call because I was in the shower, but when I called back, she didn't answer. I hoped she was okay. Brazil tried to play crazy like she wasn't feeling a nigga, but I knew she was. I mean, I listened to her please herself and scream my name.

I was on my way to her house to check on her when my phone rang. "Yo," I answered on the car phone.

"Kwame, come get me, man!" My cousin Xavier yelled through the phone.

I pulled the phone away from my ear. "I was already on my way over there to check on Zil anyway," I responded. I knew he had to be over there, because he didn't come home last night.

We had a four-bedroom condo in Novi, and we just about had enough paper to each have our own, but Zay spent most of his time over Brittany's. Me, I worked at the club we owned 'til about three AM every night, so it only made sense to live together, no point in wasting bread on two cribs.

Me and Zay been in the streets since I was about fifteen years old. My uncle died, and Zay had his mom and littles sister to feed. He met that nigga Beto, and we ain't looked back since.

We had the whole city on lock—hell, most of the East Coast. Anybody who had any good product got it from us. We were doing good for ourselves. I don't know what Zay told y'all, but we were rich as *fuck.* We owned car washes, hair salons, a restaurant, and two clubs. Yeah, we'd been through a lot, but y'all are going to have to read about that in another book. The important thing is, we deserve everything we have, and that's all facts.

He groaned. "I'm at Krystal's, man. Don't say shit, just come get a nigga. This bitch tripping and done put sugar in my tank." I already knew he was pissed after I heard *that.* It was nothing new, though. "She lucky she my baby mama, or I would beat her ass!"

Laughing, I replied, "Alright, man, here I come. You going to learn , you keep fucking with that bitch, she always on silly shit" I said.

When I pulled up to Krystal's house, Zay was outside sitting on the porch. As soon as he got up to get in my car, here came this loud-ass bitch.

I couldn't stand Krystal. We never got along, she always was being loud and acting like the hood rat she is, just like right now. All outside with these little-ass shorts and a tube top. She was yelling and screaming. I always wondered why my cousin liked this crazy-ass girl. I was a gentleman and very respectful to woman all the time, but her? She just did too much all the time.

Zay jumped into the passenger seat of my 2019 Lexus RX 350. This was my everyday car, but please believe, I had some foreign shit, too. As we pulled off, I saw Krystal still yelling at the car. We laughed at her crazy ass out there putting on a show. "Y'all must have got into it?"

"Man, she just crazy as shit," he explained, staring out the window . "She went through my phone while I was asleep, saw me texting Britt, and went crazy."

The story didn't surprise me, it happened almost every time Zay was with either Krystal or Brittany. "Why you even over here after all that shit that happen the other night?" I pointed out. "You would think you would be off her ass," I said as I pulled some weed out of my hoodie pocket and handed it to him.

He took it and started to break it up while we talked, his head pointed down at the work. "Man, I was, but I was blowing Brittany up the other night she wasn't answering or texting me back. Krystal called, I was high and drunk, I wanted some pussy, and she was offering, so you know how that go," Zay laughed as he rolled the blunt.

I didn't. "Naw, I don't know because she crazy, and you know every time you start fucking with her again, a whole bunch of shit 'bout to get started."

"Man, I ain't trying to hear that shit," Zay protested. "Let's smoke, I need to clear my head, cuz." He lit the blunt, took two hits, and passed it to me.

Zay likes all that drama shit with the hoes. Brittany and Krystal weren't the only hoes he had fighting over him, they were just the only two he cared about. He was messy. He would fuck the bottle girls that worked at our club, the hair stylists from the shop, hell, even the little hoe from around the corner.

Zay was flashy and cocky. Me, I was a behind the scenes type of guy. I was lowkey, nobody never knew who I was dating or when we broke up. I wasn't on social media blasting my relationship and all that, but Zay, that was how he got caught up most of the time.

He would be commenting on pictures, posting kissy faces and shit, he was just wild with it. Now, don't get me wrong, he loved Brittany to death like he wanted to marry her, but he wouldn't stop doing all that bullshit, so Brittany and him stayed breaking up.

We pulled up in front of Brazil's house. Zil and her sisters had money. I mean they were well off, I don't know why they wouldn't move out of the hood. I understand that was their grandma's house, but too much shit went down over here. Before I could get out the car, my trap phone rung. It was one of our workers, Moni.

I answered on the second ring. "What up, blood?"

Moni said, "The spot got hit this morning, Joe and Dough are locked up."

"FUCK, how did this happen?!" I screamed into the phone.

I told Zay what happened, and he was pissed off. We had to get Joe and Dough out of jail and find out who told on us. I knew someone was telling; we had been doing this shit for years and never got hit. Ever. We had police and judges on our payroll just so if we did ever get hot, it wouldn't be hard to get it to go away.

After all the years we been hustling, we never had anything like this happen. We moved smart. Zay might be flashy, but the way he ran his organization was smooth and under the radar. There had to be a snake in the crew somewhere, and I was going to find out who.

I may be laid back, but I was a killer, and I would kill anybody that tried to hurt me and my family. I was big on in loyalty; hell, I would die over it. I got my first body at fourteen years old.

My mama's husband used to beat her ass all the time when I was little. I say her husband, because that's who he was. He wasn't my daddy—My daddy got killed a week before I was born. My mama made sure I knew who he was and that I stayed in touch with my family. That's why me and Zay were so close: our daddies where brothers. Both of them are dead now.

One day, I came home from school and walked in on him beating on my mama again—this time he was stomping her in the face. I ran back to my room and grabbed my pistol I kept under my bed. Without hesitation, I shot him in the back of the head. As soon as he fell, I was standing over him, staring down at him with hate burning in my eyes, and shot him three more times in the face.

My mama was so fucked up she stayed in the hospital for a week, lost my baby sister, and everything. Apparently, he was mad at my mama because she didn't give him her money. I couldn't believe he would do her like that while she was carrying his child. I remember hearing my mama on the phone telling somebody she had lost a baby before; I bet it was because of his pussy ass.

After that, my nose was cut. When I started working for Beto after Zay introduced me, he had me kill a few more people and since then, I was on tip. My name was Nightmare in the street, because I was a nigga's worst

. I would rock you to sleep and then go back to my normal laid-back self.

Me and Zay pulled off, heading to our safe house on the East side of Detroit. Damn, I really needed to check on Zil, but I had to handle this shit first. I wasn't trying to kill nobody in my Mike Amiri jeans, *fuck!*

The Risks We Take for Love

Doin' our thing, movin' too fast

Candy paint with the windows all black

Seats crème brûlée, what they gon' say?

With the top down screamin', "Money ain't a thing"

We up 'til six in the mornin'

When the sun rise, we be on it

Ooh, I got five, you know it's all live

Tell me when to go, baby, when we gon' slide?

—H.E.R.

CHAPTER 12

♥**Brittany**♥

I was so sick of Zay texting and calling me all day. I was sick of Bianca and this whole trying-to-get-in-touch-with-our-mother shit. And then on top of that, my little sister had her heart broke again; I had to try to make her feel better. See, Brazil wasn't like me, she wasn't going to get Ron back how I was doing with Zay. Zil was a free spirit. She was going to meditate, burn some sage and candles, read a book, and act like she was fine, but I knew she wasn't. I need a break, man. I was the head of the family, and I had to make sure everyone was okay.

I walked into Zil's room. She was laying on her king-sized bed, reading a book, and she didn't lift her gaze up to meet me when I came in. "Zil, you okay? Tell me the truth."

Brazil sighed as she closed the novel she was reading, keeping her spot marked with a finger tucked inside. "Yeah, I guess I am, I just feel dumb, you know? I should've left when I felt his energy was off..." she answered, her face dropping further. "I knew he was up to something... He was being so clingy and annoying, I was threw off," she kept explaining.

"Yeah, sis, I know, but don't blame yourself. It ain't your fault he a fuckboy," I said, laughing.

My little sister's chest puffed out with new determination. "You right, I'm off his ass, sis, I swear."

Brazil nodded, then sighed, rubbing at her forehead. "I was so mad last night, I cried so hard all the way home, but I promise I'm good now," she said.

I was quiet for a moment, thinking, when an idea popped into my head. "Hey, let's go out tonight. I don't have to work, and we haven't been out in a long time..." I suggested to my sister. I know I was pushing it, but it was worth a try. Zil never wanted to go out, but she might be down tonight.

"You know what? Yep, let's go."

Now, I was geeked up. I was ready to party hard with my little sister. I was going to call up our cousins and we would be going to Club Spice. That was one of Zay & Kwame's club. I didn't want to see him, but that's the only club we could go to, be straight, and not have to worry about a damn thing.

A while had passed, actually, a good few hours, when Zil walked into the kitchen where I was pouring us some shots. Brazil looked bad as *fuck.* She had on a black tube top leather dress that looked painted on; it hugged all her curves. She had on a pair of strappy Saint Laurent heels, her hair was flat ironed bone-straight, and her make-up was very natural, aside from a red matte lipstick on her brown skin, which already looked like a milk Hershey bar. To finish off the look, she had a light body glitter spray that covered her, leaving her shimmering.

"Damn, Zil. You look cute as hell, sis!" I squealed as she walked up to the table and picked up a shot.

Brazil was in rare form. She was drinking, and Zil never drank anything but wine. No matter what she said, I knew my baby was going through something, and she was hurt. She tossed back the drink. "Naw, Britt, *you* look cute," Zil playfully argued.

I had on a red bodycon dress with the same Saint Laurent heels Zil had on, but mine were nude. I had wand-curled my hair, and my face was beat to the gods. I was being extra, because I knew that Zay would be in the bar that night. I had on my big diamond chain that held a blinged-out letter B with its matching bracelet. I was going to cut up tonight, just for Zay's sake, I wanted him to *know* I had been ignoring him.

****

The club was packed wall to wall, and we were in our VIP section, turning up with our cousins Amber, Kelly, and Jess. We were the baddest in the club. Keeping up with how she had been acting before we left, Zil was ordering bottles and dancing. I knew my sister was in her feelings; she was lit, dancing and popping bottles. I wish Bebe was here! She would love to see this, because she swore Zil didn't know how to have fun. Meanwhile, I had my phone out and was on Snap; I had to have proof my little sister was fun when she wanted to be.

As me and Zil danced to *All Dat* by Moneybagg Yo and Megan thee Stallion, I noticed Zay and Kwame walking into our section. That's when I really started dancing. I bent over and made my ass clap as the beat dropped. I had to be extra, because now I knew he was watching. All the while, Zil was matching my energy.

We were having a ball, and I could tell Zay was pissed by the look in his eyes. He was so fine, how could I stay mad at him forever? He was 6’2”, and his all-black Versace jean outfit was fitting his buff body just right. He had on so much jewelry he could light up the room. He followed my every move as he drank from his bottle of Ace of Spades, while I danced until the end of the song and inevitably sat down to cool off.

Zay walked up and stood in front of me. “So, you in here showing your ass tonight, huh, B?” I acted like I didn’t hear him and took a shot of D'Ussé. Suddenly, he grabbed me and pulled me so close we were almost kissing. “Stop playing with me in here, B. I will act a fool,” He whispered in my ear.

I still didn’t say anything, I just smiled and licked my lips. As I went to sit down, *City Girls Twerk* came on. This was my *jam.* I started dancing and moving to the beat as soon as Yung Miami started rapping, and I went crazy, twerking my ass. I bent over and made it clap, then I bounced one of my ass cheeks to the beat, then the other one.

I looked over to my left, and my cousins were just as lit as me. We were putting on show, all eyes were on us. To my right, I couldn’t believe my eyes, Zil was bent over in front of Kwame, making her ass bounce to the beat. I walked over to her and was geeking my sister up. We danced to about three more songs after that—I haven’t had this much fun in a long time.

▪▪▪

I was in the bathroom of the club with Zil and my cousins, and we were fixing our hair and makeup; we had been showing our asses all night. "Zil, girl, I didn't even know you knew how to dance like that," my cousin Amber said while putting nude lip gloss on.

"My baby sis was throwing ass all night," I giggled.

Zil was just standing there, brushing her hair. "Y'all crazy; I know how to dance, I just don't."

An echoing chorus of laughter followed. "Don't act like I ain't see you dancing on Kwame. Girl, you swear he be bothering you; he really going be on your head for real now," Kelly said, smiling.

Brazil gave a snort. "I'm just having fun y'all, it aint even like that." I knew she liked Kwame, she just didn't like that he was in the streets. We walked out of the bathroom, and walking in was Krystal and her friends. I didn't feel like that shit tonight. I walked past, grimed her, and kept it moving. I was looking too cute to even go there with her tonight, so we went to our section and continued to enjoy our night.

Zil was still ordering shots and dancing. She was going to pass her limit if she hadn't already. I told her to slow down, but she wasn't paying me any mind. Maybe this was a bad idea.

▪▪▪

Done with these niggas

I don't love these niggas

I dust off these niggas

Do it for fun

Don't take it personal

Personally, I'm surprised you

Called me after the things I said

—Sza

CHAPTER 13

Bianca

My sisters went out tonight. This would be the perfect time to call our mama; I didn't want them to be around or even walk past while I was talking to her. The weeks were flying by, and I had to take care of this ASAP.

Ring, Ring, Ring

An automated voice answered me instead of the familiar one I was hoping for. *"The number you have called is not in service. Please check the number and try again.*

Damn, this wasn't the right number. Now what? I have to find her before I was too far along to get an abortion! I didn't have any other options. I couldn't keep a baby. What was I going to do with a baby?! On top of that, just thinking of who my baby was by... Lord, *NO.* I had to think of something fast. Maybe I could go to the address I had for her and see if she was still there? That's what I would do. I'd have Carlos drive me there.

******

I sat in front of the small house that was supposed to be the house where my mother lived. "You ready, Bebe?" Carlos asked.

"No, but I don't have no choice but to be. I have to get this taken care of, and she's the only person that can help me," I answered as I stared at the house.

I was about to see my mother for the first time in a long time, and the only reason I was coming to see her now was because I needed this abortion. I opened the car door and got out.

"You want me to go with you?" Carlos asked.

"Naw, I got it." I responded as I walked up to the door.

Knock, Knock, Knock.

I stood there and waited. I knocked again, and still no answer. I turned to walk away, fighting back my emotions. Man, fuck, now what was I going to do? As soon as I got to the car, I heard someone call my name. I turned around, and there stood my mama.

She was still pretty like I remember, with brown skin like me and my sisters. She was way skinnier than I remembered, and she had her hair cut into a short style. "Hey, Ma," I said low as I stepped on the porch. "I need to talk to you."

What pretty features were on her face before were entirely replaced with an expression of disgust. "I ain't got no money for you. Hell, you should be giving me some. I know your sisters over there fucking on them dope boys."

I cut her off before she could get any further. "Ma, I don't need no money from you," I assured. "I do need you to do something for me, though. I can't ask Brittany or Brazil because they don't have custody of me." I braced myself for her response.

"Oh, yeah. I know they don't," she snorted, still standing in the door. Now she was smoking a joint she had pulled out of her robe pocket. "I'm not giving them bitches custody of you, I need to keep you on my case at DHS as long as I can." My head spun, and I closed my eyes as she continued. "Your sisters got all that money and won't even send me none when I call. That's the least they can do—I did give them life."

My mama was talking crazy. I never understood why she felt like my sisters owed her anything. She left us to take care of ourselves and never once came and checked on us. I don't really know the whole story about why she left us, and I really didn't care at this point. All I know is my mama was there, then one day, she wasn't.

I shook off my disbelief. "Listen, Ma. I'm pregnant, and I need to get an abortion, but I can't 'cause I'm not old enough to go alone, and I don't want to tell Brittany and Brazil because they gon' be tripping." I said everything all in one breath.

I stared at her just standing there hitting her joint, laughing. "So you mean to tell me your little hot ass done went and got pregnant, and you need me to get you an abortion?" She was still cackling. "Now why would I do that, huh? Why would I help you do something like that? You don't help me at all, you come to my doorstep and ask me something like that. What am I going to get if I help you out?"

My eyes blinked, and I opened my mouth, but what I was hearing knocked me off my feet. I grit my teeth. "What do you mean what are you going to get, I'm your daughter!"

I exploded. "You haven't done anything for me. My sisters raised me, and I never asked you for anything, the one time I need you, you can't be there for me. I knew I shouldn't have come here."

With that, I and turned and walked away.

She reached out and grabbed my arm before I could get away. "Wait, Bianca!" I wheeled around, eyes flaring with rage. "I'll do it, but you going have to give me a thousand."

Before I could go off again, she hurriedly blurted, "Listen, I haven't been working the streets like I used to, and Jake only got two other girls working. I need the money so I can take care of a few things around here. You know, bills don't pay themselves," she explained.

I couldn't believe she was trying to charge me to sign a piece of paper. It's not like I asked her to pay for it—hell, I ain't even ask her to take me, I had my own ride. I just needed her to meet me there and sign the fucking papers! I had to find another way; I wasn't about to deal with her and her sheisty ways.

But then what else choice did I have? I had to figure something out, my time was limited. "Okay, fuck it. I'll pay you the money. Do you have a number so I can call you and let you know when and where to meet me?" I sighed.

She sucked her teeth. "Yeah, but I need the money up front before we go. How I know you ain't going get me to sign for you and then run off without paying me?" my 'mother' asked.

I wanted to tear my hair out. "I need to take care of this! I'm giving you your money, Ma!" I barked back. I was tired of going back and forth with her. She had nerve. All she cared about was money and that no-good nigga Jake. I never understood her.

"Listen here, you little fast bitch!" Her milk chocolate skin was tainted with red. "I am doing something for *you*, so we going do it my way, otherwise you can get your ass from off my porch!" she screamed at me.

"Okay, okay!" I threw up my hands. "I'm not about to fight with you! I'll bring you the money in a few days and let you know when my appointment is," I snapped as I turned and walked away. I had to hurry up and get away from her. As soon as I got into the car, I burst into tears. I couldn't believe my own mother was doing this to me. She had it easy, with three kids that she didn't even have to take care of!

I could see why B and Zil didn't deal with her and why they wanted me to stay away from her now. I should've listened to them. If I would've just done what I was supposed to do, I wouldn't be in the situation I'm in now. I was going have to go into my savings and pay her. I had been putting up money for a while now, but after I paid my mama, I wasn't going to have much left. Hopefully it doesn't cost that much to get it done. I'd be fucked. Lord, if you let me get out of this, I swear I'd do what I had to do.

Los had heard the whole conversation between me and Mama. "Don't cry, Bebe," he urged. "You should've known she was going be on bullshit. Look, I got you if you need me to, but I think you should tell Marcus what is going on," he said as he pulled off.

I rubbed my face and tried to breathe. "Look, Los, thanks for being there for me, but *please,* let me handle this on my own. You promised me you wasn't going to say anything to him..." Now I was crying so hard I could barely get my words out. I was so ready for this to be over. I would be calling the clinic first thing Monday morning.

He winced. "Bebe, I'm sorry, man, calm down! I'm not going to say nothing. I got you, I swear, just stop crying," Carlos said as he reached over and hugged me. I was in my feelings about a lot of stuff. I needed to get it together.

▪▪▪

The Risks We Take for Love

Fucked her in the movies

Thumb in her booty, yeah, she nasty

I just did so she can run and tell Ashely

I want to eat it every time she walk past me

—Interstate Gotto

CHAPTER 14

Brazil

I danced all night. I was so drunk I couldn't see straight, but I felt good. I had not a worry in the world; after as many drinks as I had, I didn't care about Ron anymore. I was over it, and I wasn't looking back. Kwame was at the club tonight, and since he walked in, I had been by his slide like I was his girl.

Now, y'all know I'm a very laid-back person, but tonight, I was in rare form. I had downed so many shots and drunk so much Ace of Spades, I felt like a whole different person. Me, B, Kelly, Amber, and Jess were the baddest chicks in the club. I had just got off the dance floor from dancing to Juvenile's *Back That Thang Up.*

Yeah, I know it was old, but nobody could resist dancing when that one came on. I sat down on the all-white leather couch with sliver trim, and Kwame walked up and sat down next to me. Man, he was looking so good tonight. He had on an all-black, Purple Brand jean outfit, and his dreads were pulled up into a messy man bun.

He didn't have on much jewelry tonight, just a simple chain with a charm shaped like a 'K' with his iced-out Rolex, and his Buffs tucked inside his shirt. He picked up a shot and handed it to me, and then grabbed up one for himself, then he leaned in close to me so we could toast our glasses.

I took the shot and watched him drink from the bottle of Ace he had in is hand. Man, his pink lips and light green eyes were making my panties soaked. *Please Me* by Bruno Mars and Cardi B started playing, and I began dancing to the beat in my seat.

I felt him watching me. He handed me another shot and I took it as I continued to sway to the beat. Without any encouragement, I stood up and continued to dance. I felt Kwame's hands grab me around my waist and pull me into his lap.

Before he could even get adjusted to my weight, I started giving him a lap dance, grinding myself and twerking in his lap. As I rolled my hips, I felt his lips kissing on my neck. He placed soft smooches all down my throat and up to my ear; my body was heating up. I don't know what was happening to me, but I was painfully turned on by his touch.

Looking for something to ground me, I snatched his bottle and took a drink. I was past my limit and feeling myself while his hands were rubbing up my thighs. The more he touched on me, the more I rolled my hips in his lap. The song had went off, and I still was sitting in his lap, grinding.

We were in our own little world. Even though I knew I didn't need any more to drink, I took another shot. It was starting to make me feel sick, but I was holding it together. Wobbling, I stood up to look for my sister, my eyes scanning the crowd.

And then there he was. Ron, standing at the bar.

As soon as I saw him, it's like I wasn't even drunk anymore. I knew he saw me too, because our eyes locked, and he looked like he had seen a ghost. I knew I couldn't let him think he ran me out, so I turned up some more! I grabbed Kwame's hand and pulled him to the dance floor.

I was all over him—I mean, you would've thought we were fucking with how I was dancing on him. My hands wrapped around his wrists to rest his on my ass as I moved to the music. Kwame was kissing my skin all over and feeling me up. To my delight, after looking up, I saw Ron's eyes glued to us from where he sat the bar.

I grabbed Kwame and pressed my lips into his soft pink ones. Yes, I was doing this because I was drunk and wanted to make Ron mad. I wanted to hurt him like he hurt me. But y'all already knew I couldn't wait to feel Kwame's lips on mine. I had been dreaming about this.

I never showed Kwame any play because I didn't like what he did for a living, but I would be lying if I said I didn't like him. I mean, come on; I masturbated to the thought of him touching me.

"I'm ready to go, Kwame. Can you drive me home? I'm drunk and I'm ready to leave..." I whispered in his ear.

His hand rubbed from my hip up towards the small of my back. "Zil, I have to close up tonight, I told Zay I would. But you can go lay down in my office 'til I'm done and then I will," he suggested. Rubbing my eye with the heel of my hand, I nodded.

I knew my sister and everyone else would be ready to go at this point, but the drinks were starting make my head spin. I pulled out my phone and sent the girls a text in a group message:

Me: Im going to lay down in Kwame's office and he is goin to take me home after he close up.

Britt: Aw shit Zill giving up that pussy tonight!

Amber: lol bout time

Kelly: Get it Zil

Jess: I seen Ron Zil I know u did that's why u was dancing with Kwame like that?

Me: Im NOT A HOE LIKE YALL LOL. Im drunk and I don't want to ruin y'all night so im gon lay down, thats all. yall have fun. Oh yea, btw, I seen Ron's bitch Ass fuck him

Britt: Okay Sis, ill see you when I get home. I love you Zil and im glad you came out tonight. You deserve to enjoy yourself.

Smiling to myself, I put my phone in my purse and grabbed Kwame's hand so I could follow him upstairs to his office. The view from the wide windows that made up the accent walls was amazing. On one side, you could see the whole downtown Detroit, and then the other side looked down into the club.

The office was as big as a studio apartment. The back of the room held an enormous black glass desk with a big leather chair. Everything opposite it looked like a living room. It was furnished with a couch that matched the shade of the desk with gold throw pillows and a luxurious, fluffy, black and gold blanket.

On the floor, there was an antique Russian rug with a glass coffee table that must have come in a set with the desk, which was adorned with neat papers in a small stack placed to the side. A bookshelf with a lot of different of books flanked it, and curious, I walked over and noticed one of my favorite books, *A Broken Heart Still Beats* by Miz Lala. “I didn’t know you read,” I noted as I picked up the book and opened it up. It was autographed by Miz Lala herself.

Kwame walked up behind me and put his arms around my waist. “Yeah, I love to read. That’s one of my favorites,” he admitted after looking at the title of the novel in my hands.

I set it down, turning around to stare deeply into his light green eyes. “Wow, one of mine too...” He was still hugging me, so he didn’t have far to go when he leaned in close and kissed me on my cheek, then my neck, and then down my chest. I was getting hot; I could feel my thong getting soaked from my own juices.

I pulled away so I could walk over to the small bar and pour me a shot. When I looked up again, he was now sitting on the couch. He had taken off his jean jacket and his tight

V-neck hugged his buff body. Oh my God, Kwame was so fine, Lord.

"You want a shot?" I asked as I poured another one.

He looked up, cocking an eyebrow. "Yeah, sure, but I don't think you need any more, Brazil," Kwame warned, watching me with concern I didn't register.

Laughing and brushing off the suggestion, I handed him his shot and took another one. "I'm good, Kwame." I tried to walk back to the bar and almost fell. Yeah, I think I might need to stop drinking tonight.

Kwame waved his hand for me to join him. "Come sit down, Brazil." When I took the spot next to him, the smell of Jimmy Cho filled my nose; my head was spinning. Kwame's hand was rubbing on my thigh, and I didn't make him stop.

He leaned in and kissed my lips, so I returned the favor. Our tongues danced as we made out, and the whole time, he let his hands explore all over my body. He pulled my hips on top of his and continued to let his tongue run over mine.

Part of me knew I was letting him kiss me because I was drunk. I shouldn't be doing this; I just broke up with Ron, and I wasn't even over it yet—but Kwame kissing and touching me felt so good. I had dreamed about this moment more than once.

He broke our lip-lock to begin placing kisses on my neck and down my chest. When he got to my breasts, I held my breath and pulled he pulled them out. It came out of me as soft moan when he took my nipple into his warm mouth.

He flicked his tongue over and over across the left bud and rolled the right one in between his fingers. I closed my eyes and let his touch take all the pain I was feeling about Ron away. Before I knew it, he pulled his T-shirt over his head, and placed my legs over his shoulders.

Kwame kissed me in between my legs and all over my stomach. “Take this dress off, Brazil,” he whispered in my ear. I did what I was told, then got back in the position he had placed me in before I took my dress off.

In just a black thong, Kwame kept up his efforts to leave my skin stained with bruise-like hickeys, taking his fingers and parting my spilt while he sucked and nibbled on my thigh. I was *dripping* wet; to the point where my juices were running down my leg. He rubbed my clit in tender circles with the pad of his thumb, and then I felt his wet, warm tongue enter me. I never had head before, and I don’t understand why I waited so long. I was in a trance.

Now, I've came before, but I never made myself feel how I was feeling right now. I don’t know if it was the liquor or if it was just him, but it didn’t matter now. Kwame ate me like I was his last meal.

I felt myself reaching the point of no return. I was shaking, and a cold air filled my whole body. Next thing I knew, I was coming so hard my legs shook, and Kwame drank every drop. After I finished, I thought he was going to stop, but he kept going, feasting on me like I was the best thing he ever tasted. Once it was over, I had gotten off four times and I never felt so good.

Kwame came up to press his lips to mine, and I kissed him like I never kissed anyone before. “Damn, Brazil. You taste good as fuck," he complimented as he got up to take a shot D'Ussé.

I was just lying there naked, watching him with half-lidded eyes. After all of that excitement and alcohol, I was drunk and exhausted. I pulled the fluffy blanket over my body, and Kwame walked back over to the couch and laid down next to me. "Brazil, I have to go downstairs and collect all the money we made tonight and, update the books and then I will take you home, if that's cool?" he asked.

I stirred awake from my half-conscious daze. "Yeah, that's fine, as long as you stay with me, and we do what we just did again..." I mumbled as my eyes closed slowly.

"What we did?" Kwame laughed. "You mean what I did," he corrected, walking out of his office.

All I got is these broken clocks

I Ain't got no time

Just burning day light

Still love, and it's still love, and it's still love

It's still love, but it's still love

Nothin' but love for you

—Sza

CHAPTER 14

I had a ball last night. I really enjoyed myself, and Zil got out and let her hair down, which was really a plus. I never seen my sister dance so much, but the craziest part was that she left with Kwame.

Ring, ring, ring!

I pushed Zay in his side to wake him up, groaning. I know I told y'all I wasn't fucking with him, and I really tried to ignore him all last night, but I couldn't. He was looking so good, and then I saw Krystal and her crew walk in, so I had no other choice.

"Zay!" The phone was still blaring away, and all I could do was pull my pillow over my head. "Your phone been ringing all morning, would you answer it or put it on DND. Damn, I got a headache!" I yelled at him, because he was acting like he couldn't hear that ringer going off for the last two hours.

I knew it had to be Krystal blowing up his phone, because she had seen me leave with Zay last night. Kwame was closing the club, so we left a little after Zil went to lay down; it wouldn't have been one of them.

I checked my phone just to be sure, and man, I had so many missed calls from Passion. She had caught sight of me last night at the club too. Unfortunately, her and Krystal were sisters. I know what you're thinking, but if it means anything, I didn't know that was her sister until we had already fucked. By that time, it was too late.

Passion was cool for the most part; we did our thing when we wanted to, mostly after a good night of drinking and making money. Sometimes, she would get jealous if she caught me talking to another girl or guy. She *hated* Zay. For one, she didn't like how he played her sister, and for two, because she hated that I wouldn't leave him alone.

I know this shit was messy, but there wasn't anything I could do about it now. I planned on leaving Passion alone completely a month ago; y'all see I didn't. With raised eyebrows, I read through all the text messages she sent. She was tripping, saying she would tell Zay and Krystal about us. I really didn't care if she did, to be honest, I just knew it was going to cause more problems than I felt like dealing with.

"Zay, get up. I'm 'bout to shower and I want to go get breakfast." Looking in his phone and reading all his texts, he nodded his head yeah absently.

I went into my bathroom. I had the master bedroom and bath in our house, while Zil and Bebe shared the other. I stepped inside my standup shower, and the water ran down my whole body. I had a slight hangover, but the water was making me feel a little bit better.

My hair was in a body wave sew-in that Zil had done for me a week ago, and even though I had just wand-curled it last night, I didn't care that it was getting wet. I grabbed the mango butter scented Dove Instant Body Foam and pumped some on my rag, using it to wash up about four times.

Once I finished rinsing off, I stepped out and wrapped a XXL Polo towel around my body, then walked out into my bathroom. Zay was on the phone, arguing with Krystal about coming to pick up Demi Rose. She knew he was here, and that it would be a problem because she didn't want Demi around me. Despite that, I had enjoyed my night and I was in a good mood, besides a little headache. As I got dressed, I listened to what he was saying to her.

"Krystal, I'm comin' to pick my baby up in an hour. We going to go to breakfast. So, get her dressed." I don't know why he said that. All you could hear was her going crazy from his end of the phone.

I put on my black Nike sports bra, some runner shorts to match and brushed my deep wave bundles into a neat bun. I walked over to Zay while he was still holding the phone and wrapped my arms around his neck from behind. "I'm ready to go to breakfast!" I knew she heard me, because as soon as I said that, she was screaming at the top of her lungs

I heard her ranting over the phone. She didn't sound too pleased. "You thought you and that hoe was 'bout to play family with my baby, you got me fucked up Xavier." Then, there was no response on the other line. She had hung up. I knew she was going to do that. Now, don't get me wrong, I loved Demi Rose, it wasn't like I was trying to push them apart or anything. I mean, we all know Krystal wasn't going to let him come get his kid. She just wanted him to stop hanging around over here with me.

I'd been around Demi before. That was when Krystal had a boyfriend for about six months. The whole time she was with him, Demi was with me or Zay. I learned to love that little girl. For a four-year-old, she was incredibly smart. Yeah, Zay had her on me when we first got together. She had caramel skin, long black thick hair and deep dimples. She really didn't look like Zay to me, but she didn't look like Krystal either. She did favor his little sister, though.

Zay and I were on the freeway heading downtown. It was so hot already and it wasn't even 12:00 P.M yet. The sun was shining so bright, I needed to go grab myself a Pepsi and get a stand back. Once I ate, I knew that I would start to feel better.

Times like this when me and Zay were just chilling and not fighting made me remember why I was in love with him. Zay really was my best friend. After all the drama, we really got along and matched each other perfectly.

Zay held me down when shit was hard, and he never once felt like I owed him anything. He had a lot of messy shit going on with his baby mama, but who doesn't? I know people might think I'm tripping, but I can't help how I feel about him. I really wish he could get his shit together so we could be a power couple. I had a few things I needed to handle, but it wouldn't be any trouble for me to stop talking to people.

We pulled up in front of The Hudson Café on Woodward. Zay got out and walked around to my side, then opened my door, taking my hand and helping me out of my seat. See what I mean? He could be the perfect gentleman. We walked in hand-in-hand. Oh, he could be so sweet.

As we were being seated, he walked up and pulled my chair out for me. I ordered the red velvet pancakes, eggs, bacon and a hot bowl of fruit. Zay ordered the same thing but with cinnamon roll pancake. We were enjoying our food, when someone walked up and tapped me. I looked up from my food and right into Passion's eyes.

I knew she was going to be on her bullshit, so I played it cool. "Hey Brittany. I been texting you, girl," Passion 'casually' chided as she sat down next to me. "What's up, Zay?" She called out to him, and then went back to talking to me. "So, yeah, B, I been texting you. I seen you in the club last night, girl. You left so fast we couldn't even have a drink."

I leaned back and grabbed at my plate, responding back to her, "I was so drunk that I had to leave," I explained as I put a forkful of eggs in my mouth.

"Well, do you want to practice our stage show today?" Passion asked while licking her lips.

I knew what she really wanted.

Looking up from my food, I cleared my throat. "Yeah, we can. Passion I'm kind of busy, so can I call you later?" I pointed over to Zay.

"Oh yeah, I see. Well, my sister's on her way in, so I don't think y'all going to be busy for long." Passion walked away after that.

As soon as she did, here came Krystal. I couldn't wait to get the fuck out of this little-ass city. Everywhere I went, I bumped into this hoe. I was over it. Zay and I were having a good time until her and her messy-ass sister came in. I was ready for shit to go left.

"So, you didn't pick my baby up so you could take this bitch out to breakfast!?" Krystal was yelling and causing a scene like always.

I continued to eat my food and watched her put on a show. Zay was barking back now. "Krystal, I told you I was going to come get her, but you act like I can't have her around my girl!"

Krystal laughed as she walked closer to Zay. "Your girl? Oh, that's your girl now!?"

He was getting mad now. "Krystal, please don't start shit this morning. You need to grow up."

I was done with my food and ready to go, and I wasn't afraid to cut off this silliness before it could escalate any further. "Zay, I'm ready to go." I said, standing up from the table.

Zay grabbed my hand, and we started heading for the door. "Bet, Bae we gone." As expected, she came walking after us. I really didn't want to fight today, but I know this bitch would keep just going and going and going. She lived for this shit, and I wish she would just find a nigga already. Then she would be somewhere else minding her own business and not worried about us—or even Demi Rose.

"Krystal, we are not about to do this today, okay? I'm gonna be out to pick up my baby in a few hours. You really need to chill out, you're always on some bullshit," Zay chided as we walked out of the restaurant.

I looked back and could see Passion shaking her head with this dumb look on her face. I was going to be forced to cut all that mess off with her. I might not even do our stage show with her anymore.

I know what you're thinking. Why stop fucking with her? You know Zay's not going to stop doing him. That wasn't the issue. What me and Passion were doing was messy, and she was starting to get too clingy and needy. I didn't need that.

She would text me and tell me she loved me and that she wished she could be my girl. That's especially what I didn't need right now. I didn't want a girlfriend, and I didn't even like girls like that. I just was having fun. Don't get me wrong, we vibed well together, but Passion had some messy ways, just like her sister.

I was in the truck waiting while Zay and Krystal argued in front of the building. You know what? I was over this shit. I'm telling Zay that I was done and that I meant it this time. I mean, hell, I'm sitting in the car while my so-called nigga fights with his baby mama, yet again spending more time on her than on me. He was showing her too much attention for my liking. How did my day end up going downhill? It seemed like every time him and I were doing good, she came with some bullshit to throw us off. I was tired of going through this with him. I deserved better.

Try'na get back to all my old ways

Try'na get back to all the hobbies from my old days

Try'na forget all the unnecessary

Thoughts from my head, man, it was pretty scary

—Kehlani

CHAPTER 15

Bianca

I had been up at Northland Family Planning Center waiting on my mama for about an hour. I'd been making sure I talked to her every day up until my appointment. I've had the thousand for her that I got after I went to see her for a few days now. My appointment was in about forty-five minutes, and she still had not shown up. I was calling her phone over and over, and I went past her house on the way here. Jake said that she had left already to come meet me. I can't believe that she was doing this to me. Wait—yes, I could. Mama never was there for me, so why would she be here now?

An hour later, she pulled up high as a kite. "Bianca, come on girl, lets hurry up and do this so I can go." My mama was yelling and banging on the window of Carlos' car. I opened the car door and got out. "Oh, you think you cute?" she snapped and smacked me on my ass.

"No, I don't. I think I'm irritated and sick of waiting on you. You was supposed to be here an hour ago!" I yelled back at her. I was so mad at her right now. I hoped they would still let me get it done. I was so ready to get this over with and get back to my regular life. I was so sick every morning, and it was hard hiding it from my sisters.

I walked in and checked in with the nurse at the front desk. She said I was late, but they would still see me because they were not that busy today. I was relieved, because I was desperately ready to get things over with. I took the clipboard and filled out all the papers, then handed it to my mama. She had three forms to fill out, and then she could leave. I could see now why my sisters didn't fuck with her.

"I got to fill out all this? This too much." She complained as she filled out the papers. She handed me back the clipboard.

I got up and took it back to the nurse, then went and sat back next to my mama. "Once they call my name, you can leave. My best friend's outside waiting, so I'm good."

My mom scoffed down at me. "Girl, I was leaving anyway. I'm not 'bout to sit up in here with you all day." Her words were slurred. I was starting to really not like her now. Before, I didn't really know about all the stuff she did. I heard stories, but never experienced them firsthand. She left when I was about six years old, and I didn't go through things like my sisters did. I see why Brittany said we were better off without her. All she cared about was money and obviously getting high now.

I waited about twenty minutes before my name was called. Then I stood up and hurried to grab my purse. "Okay, Mama, you can leave. I'm good," I told her as I walked towards the back of the office.

"'Bout damn time, I was ready to go when I got here. If you'd have sat your fast ass down somewhere, we wouldn't have to be wasting so much of my time," she hissed on her way out of the office. I was terribly relieved that part was over. Now to get the last of it taken care of, and I would be good. I was tired of hiding from my sisters. I hate to say it, but they were right. I should have slowed down, now look at me. Asking a woman who doesn't even care about me for help, and the only way she was willing to do it was for me to pay her.

The nurse took my vitals, and my blood pressure was high at 150/102 I'd never had high blood pressure before. The nurse told me it might be nerves and that they would give me some time to calm down. If it was still up the next time they checked, I was going to have to come back.

She gave me an ultrasound and told me that I was fifteen weeks. I don't understand how I was fifteen weeks, I should only be like 7 or 8 weeks . Omg this might be Marcus baby . I had so many thoughts going through my head. Finding out how far along I was for real , gave me a whole other feeling . But still didn't need a baby. I had to shake this . I was cutting it close, but this was my only shot. I had to get this done today, and fast. They sat me in a room to watch a video and read a book. About forty-five minutes had passed and the nurse came in to take my blood pressure again. "Bianca, honey, your blood pressure is still high. I'm sorry, but we won't be able to do the procedure today. Why don't you come back next week?"

I couldn't believe what I was hearing. I burst into tears. "I have to do this today! I have to!" I was devastated.

"Baby, please calm down, you're going to make your blood pressure go up even more." The nurse pulled me into a hug. "I'm going to go get your mother, okay?" she offered, trying her best to comfort me.

"She left, but my best friend is outside. I'm okay, I'm going to just go. Thank you so much for your help." I wiped my face with the arm of my Nike hoodie and walked away.

When I got into Carlos' car, he was asleep. He stirred eventually, and lifted himself up to look at me. "Aww, Bebe. Was it that bad?" he asked as he reached over to hug me.

"I couldn't get it, Carlos, they said my blood pressure was too high. She took it twice, forty-five minutes apart." I was crying again. "What am I supposed to do now? They want me to come back in a week or two, and I'm already fifteen weeks in."

Carlos frowned at me and turned towards the dashboard. "Dang, Bebe, I'm so sorry you going through this man. You know I got your back, no matter what." He started the car up and pulled out of the parking lot. I was so upset. I had to figure out another way to do this in two weeks. There was no way my mama was going to come back up here. Hell, it was hard enough getting her here this time. I had to figure this out before it was too late.

I gave you everything that every man say he wants

I cooked, I cleaned, I ironed your jeans, I was the one

I would listen to you when you sounded stupid

Treated you like a winner even when you were losing,

Now you got me feeling like shooting cupid

—Ella Mai

CHAPTER 16

Brazil

Ron had been blowing me up since the other night at the club. I had blocked him, but he was using a Text Now app and was changing his number over and over. It was getting a little sad. I had cried about it, been mad about it, and even got drunk about it. Now I was over it. Like, REALLY over it. I should've broken things off a long time ago.

It's all over now and to be honest I felt like a weight had been lifted off my shoulders. I really think me spending the night with Kwame was another reason I was getting over Ron, but I was happy for the relief, however it came.

I know I was drunk the other night, but I remember everything that happened. I don't regret any of it. I was sick of everyone acting like I always had to be a good girl all the time. Ron was texting me like crazy, in his feelings about Kwame, but I didn't care. Men always do stuff to women that they know they couldn't take if it was done to them. Being with Kwame made me remember my worth.

Now don't get me wrong, I know Kwame was a hood nigga. When he was with me though, he was the perfect gentleman; he acted like I was the only woman in the room.

He gave me feelings I never felt for Ron. Every time I thought about him , I got butterflies.

Ron and I had done this back and forth before. He cheated before, and I forgave him. I sometimes thought it was my fault that he cheated because I wasn't having sex with him. I just wasn't ready. I know what you're thinking. Like, how she wasn't ready to have sex with the boyfriend that she had for years, but she took it almost all the way with Kwame? I don't even know how to explain it myself. It could be because Kwame wasn't trying to force it on me—he just let the night flow.

I was meeting my sisters at LeCulture for lunch. It had been a few days since I had seen Brittany and come to think of it, I hadn't seen Bianca around much either. It was summer and I was at the shop most of the time, but it wasn't like BeBe to miss an appointment to get her hair touched up. She had not even asked me anything about getting her hair done.

I was in a good mood today. It was ninety-five degrees out, and I had just done my last head till later this evening .I was done cleaning up, I went home to shower and to change. I put on a light pink two-piece set of biker shorts, some all-white UGG sandals, and wore my hair in a low ponytail. Before leaving, I grabbed my white YSL crossbody and matching sunglasses.

As I was sitting at the table reading my Kindle, Brittany walked up and hugged me from behind. "Hey Sister, wassup?" She sat down across from me, looking cute as always. She had on a pair of high-waisted red jeans, a white crop top, and a blue jean jacket, along with our favorite

Jordan 1s. I noticed her long bundles were flat ironed bone-straight instead of the curls she had put them into before. We sat and talked for a while waiting on Bianca to get there.

Eventually, B texted and told us to order without her, as she was running behind. "So, Britt, what's been up?" I asked my sister as I took a sip of my strawberry lemonade.

"Nothing much, Zil. Been working and me and Zay been kicking it. We doing good this week." We both laughed. They were so up and down, one week they were about to kill each other, and the next they'd be in love, and you couldn't get them off each other.

"Soooo, what happened with you and Kwame?" Brit asked me, smiling.

"Nothing happened. We went to his office, I laid down until he closed the club and then we went to the house. He stayed the night and that was all." I turned the page on my book.

She sighed, sagging over dramatically in her disappointment. "Girl, you crazy. Kwame's fine as hell, and the way you was dancing on him, I just knew y'all was going to fuck."

I wrinkled my nose at her. "That's all we were doing was dancing!" I bristled, even though I wasn't entirely telling the truth. "Girl, I wasn't 'bout to fuck him!"

Her arms folded, and she stuck up her chin at me. "You should've then," she argued. "You would really be over Ron's lame ass"

"I'm over Ron," I snorted, then took a drink of my water.

Her brow cocked in skepticism. "So, you mean to tell me as drunk as you was, and as fine as Kwame is, ain't nothing happen? Wow child, you better than me!" Brittany was fanning herself.

I wanted to tell her about me and Kwame's night, but then again, I wasn't ready to either. I really didn't know how I felt about Kwame yet, and I know my sister, she was going to be doing the most. I just changed the subject. "Anyway..." I trailed off. "I wonder what's up with Bianca. She been being real weird lately."

Brittany nodded, knitting her brows. "Yeah, she be asleep when I leave for work and asleep when I come home," she agreed. You could tell she was worried about Bianca. "I hope she ain't did no dumb shit and got pregnant."

My eyes went wide. "Don't say that, B! How could she be pregnant when she not even fucking?" I pointed out, giving my sister the dumb look.

"Come on, Zil," she snorted. "You know damn well Bianca's fucking. Just because she ain't come to us and say it don't mean it's not happening. She moving just how I was moving when I started fucking."

I knew my little sister was fast, but I really hope what Brittany was saying was her just over-exaggerating. I kept a close watch on Bianca, and I tried my best to make sure she was doing what she was supposed to do.

A few minutes later our food was arriving to the table and in comes Bianca dressed like it wasn't almost a hundred degrees outside. She looked a mess; she had on an oversized Nike jogging suit with the hoodie zipped up, and her hair was pulled back lazily into a low ponytail. As soon as she walked in, I knew something was off.

Brittany got straight to the point. “Hey, Bebe, what’s up with you?”

“Hey y’all. Nothing is up with me, what’s up with y’all?” Bianca reached her hand into my plate and grabbed a wing. I had ordered the Culture Wings for an appetizer, and the ribeye with roasted carrots and whipped potatoes as my main dish. Brittany got the salmon tower, and we ordered for Bianca, who got her the lamb chops.

“Girl, if you don’t eat your own food. Damn.” We began to eat. I was watching Bianca hard, and she was scarfing her food down like this was her last meal. We ate quietly for about twenty minutes, then, out of nowhere, Brittany just blurted out, “So, Bebe, you pregnant?” My eyes got big. I looked over at Bianca and almost choked.

A small huff escaped her. “Why would you ask me something like that, Britt? Where that come from? You crazy.” Bianca kept eating and never made eye contact with me or Brittany.

Britt put her fork down. “Girl, you can pull that shit on Zil, but not on me. I knew when you started fucking, you didn’t have to tell me,” she retorted, pointing at our younger sister.

I knew this wasn’t going to end well, because both Bianca and Brittany have the worst attitude. I was just trying to enjoy my lunch and spend time with my sisters, but I should’ve known it was going to turn into a big ass argument.

Bianca drank some of her Pepsi. “Girl, go head on with that shit. I’m not pregnant, are you pregnant?” she snorted.

"Naw, I'm not!" Brittany was getting louder and louder. "I just got my Depo shot last week!"

This was humiliating. "Y'all, don't do this in this restaurant—we can talk about this when we get home," I urged, trying to calm them down.

Brittany lowered her voice. "Okay, look. I'm sorry for saying that, but on the real, what's up with you, Bebe?"

Our younger sister just sat there, looking down. She began to quietly cry. "Aww, Bebe, what's wrong?" I put my arm around her, pulling her into a hug. She was talking and crying at the same time, we couldn't understand a thing she was saying.

"Bebe, slow down, we don't understand nothing you're saying." Brittany walked our side of the table and hugged me and our baby sister. Bianca was wiping her face, trying to calm down. She took a drink of water and pulled herself together, so we all got back in our seats and just sat there looking at each other.

"Okay, Brittany, Brazil. Listen. Let me just say what I have to say, then y'all can talk," she explained, wiping her eyes with her sleeve. "It's already hard enough, and I just want to get it all out at one time, okay?"

Me and Brittany nodded our head yes. Bianca told us everything, from her being pregnant to what went down with our mother. When she was done talking, no one said anything, we just kept trying to eat and steal glances at each other.

I didn't know what to say. I was so disappointed in my sister, but I also was hurt for her that our mother treated her the way she did. Me and Brittany tried our best to make sure

Bianca never got hurt by our mother. After Mama left, that was the last time she was going to make our little sister cry.

I was scared of what Brittany was going to say. To my surprise, she didn't say anything at all. She just ate her meal and kept her mouth shut. Never in my life had I seen her speechless. Never. On top of everything, I also felt like I failed Bebe. How could this happen? What were we going to do?

There were so many thoughts going through my head, but I just sat there and didn't say a word. I had to let it sink in. I wish she would've just told us from the jump. I think I was madder about our mother then I was about her getting pregnant. We ordered a black bottom cheesecake and shared it as we talked a little bit about everything but what we needed to talk about. Once we were done, we paid the bill and got up to leave. Carlos had dropped Bebe off, so she asked if she could ride home with Brittany.

I had three more heads to do today, so I headed to the shop. It was gonna be a long day, and I was tired already. I pulled up and parked in front of the building , Y'all wouldn't believe who was parked in the spot next to me . Ron. God damn, could my afternoon get any worse?

▪▪

From the dope spot, with the smoke Glock

Fleein' the murder scene, you know me well

From nightmares of a lonely cell, my only hell

But since when y'all niggas know me to fail?

—*JAY Z*

CHAPTER 17

Xavier

I called a meeting at the warehouse. It had been around three weeks and about five of my houses had been raided by the police. I didn't have any damn idea where all this was coming from. I never had problems with the police—hell, I had a few of them on my payroll, just to try to avoid any of this from happening.

I was lucky that they had hit the houses before it was re-up time, they really didn't find anything but some money and a few guns. My workers they took to jail were all clean and nobody opened their mouth, so they were released after seventy-two hours. The police weren't looking for them in particular, so they weren't going to hold them too long.

I had to get to the bottom of this, there's a reason that police were on me so hard. We were having the meeting at our warehouse, not for the location, but because it was the only place where all my men could fit at one time. You had to remember, I own most of the blocks on Detroit's East and West side.

Almost everybody was here; I was missing about four men, but as soon as everyone was there, I would begin. I even invited Javier. Although he was in charge of the West Coast, we still were part of the same team, and if they were gunning for me, sooner or later they would be looking at Javier too.

He walked in the warehouse dressed just like his dad, in a pair of black dress pants and a linen button-up Fendi shirt, with the loafers to match. "Mi hermano!" The two of us embraced. Now, don't get me wrong, me and Javier bumped heads a lot—he was always in is feelings—but I loved him. We got a lot of money together, and I promised Beto that I was going to look after him.

When everyone was accounted for, Kwame started the meeting. "Now, we all know why we are here. A few of our spots have got hit in the past few weeks. We don't know where its coming from, but we are going to find out," he said firmly, scanning the crowd for any glimpses of fear before continuing.

"We never had problems with the police before, but something had to have happened for them to be on our backs like this," Kwame explained. "So does anybody have anything they have to tell us about?"

No one said anything, they all just looked around, dumb and confused. I had a way of reading people, and from the looks of it, it seemed that everyone was solid. I didn't see anybody moving around or avoiding making eye contact with me or Kwame. "Okay well since no one seems to know what brought all this attention on us, we going have to switch shit up a little bit," I cut in.

They all looked up, and since I had everyone's attention, I laid down the law. "All the houses are shut down until further notice. We will let y'all know when to start up again and where you'll be working when we open back up. So, for now, y'all just chill and lay low."

A chorus of bitching and moaning from the crowd followed my words. “Man, how long we going be on chill?” demanded one of our workers named Chip, the only one out of the group brave enough to speak to me directly.

“As long as I want y’all to be on chill.”

His face immediately went red. “Man, Zay I can’t just be chilling. I got eight kids; I need to be working! I need the money!”

I was getting irritated with this nigga. “So you mean to tell me you don’t got no bread saved up with as good as I pay y’all?!” I yelled so that everybody could hear me. “I don’t want nobody complaining about us being shut down since don’t nobody know what’s going on! ‘Cause of that, we have to do it this way, otherwise how am I gonna get rid of the problem?”

I didn’t have time to hear all these niggas bitching about this, so I made sure everyone understood what I was saying; I hated repeating myself. Kwame always led the meetings because he said I was rude and didn’t know how to talk to my employees. I didn’t give a fuck though—these niggas acted like they were doing me a favor.

Don’t get me wrong, they did hold it down, but there was always a young nigga looking to be part of my team. If anyone had a problem with how I talked or ran my operation, they could and would be replaced.

We told them they could leave, and everyone milled out of the warehouse, except me, Kwame, and Javier. I wasn’t looking forward to it, but I needed to ask them what they really thought was going on.

I normally would have an idea or a gut feeling when something wasn't going right, but right now, I was lost and couldn't put my finger on what was going on. "So, Javier. Did you notice any one acting funny or looking weird during the meeting?"

"No realmente, mi hermano, I really didn't," he admitted. Something was clearly bugging him, though. His attention swiveled over towards Kwame briefly, then back to me. "But, the one chico who spoke up 'bout you shutting everything down? You need to get rid of him."

Kwame sucked his teeth, his way of showing disapproval at the suggestion. "Man, Zay you know how he is. He got all of them baby mamas on his head about that money," he piped up, cutting Javier off. They really didn't get along. I mean me and Javier didn't either, but this wasn't a party; it wasn't about who we enjoyed being around, **it** was about getting this money and making sure everything ran smooth.

"Listen, Xavier," Javier insisted. "You need to cut that Chico loose—he is questioning the decisions you make for your organization. That means he is questioning you as a boss." I wanted to sigh. This was just dumping more on my plate. "You don't need no one working for you that think the choices you make are not smart. All your men need to fall in line and not question authority."

The two of them exchanged firm stares. "Zay, you know he just wanted to know how long it was gonna be, I don't think he was questioning your authority, but just asking a question that all of them were thinking," Kwame explained to me, going against Javier.

"Y'all, don't start that shit, man!" I finally cut them off, rubbing my temples. "I got **to many** other things to worry about. Like, why the fuck the police on my back so hard? I talked to my officers I got on payroll, and they haven't heard anything about it," I barked.

Now I was pacing, trying to get my thoughts together. "I need to get to the bottom of this shit before the new shipment is ready." Finally looking up at the two of them after gathering myself, I was satisfied that they had both dropped the debate. "Javier, are you going to Mexico this week or next week for our monthly check in?"

He nodded. "I'mma go this week and get it over with. You should come too and let them know what's going on with the police, you would hate them to find out from someone else," Javier grimly laughed. "Then we gon' have bigger problems."

Beto had made sure I was locked in with all these people before he got sick, and most of the time, me and Javier took turns going to see them, but he was right; if they heard about everything going on from someone else, it would be bad. They would cut me off thinking I was hiding something, and more importantly, they would cut my supply off.

It wouldn't even matter that Beto was their brother. There were rules you had to follow, and it didn't matter who you were or who blessed you in. If you didn't obey by the rules, then it was a wrap. No talking.

I really hated the fact I had to go see these people and didn't have an explanation for them on what was going on. I had planned on going to see them after I figured out what was going on, who was behind it, and had already taken care of it. "Fuck. Man, I guess you right. I wasn't trying to go see them just yet, but I rather they hear it from me than anyone else," I admitted with a sigh.

After we wrapped up our little meeting and set a date and time to meet up to leave for Mexico, Javier was on his way, and I could focus on my regular life again. Krystal had been blowing my phone up all day, texting all kinds of wild shit. Man, she never understood when I told her I was working.

I was going to pick up my daughter today. I hadn't spent that much time with her in a while. I didn't give a fuck what Krystal was talking about, I was gonna get her and take her with me for a few days. Being with my baby girl was the only thing that was going get my mind off all the bullshit that was going on. She was my outlet from the real world.

Brittany was too, but things have been rocky between us. I know y'all thinking it's my fault, but I got a feeling Brittany been on some bullshit too. Now I don't know with who, because I run these Detroit Streets and every nigga through this bitch knows Brittany my girl, so it couldn't be nothing serious.

I pulled up to Krystal's house and there were about four cars parked out front. You could hear the music playing loud from outside, too. See, this is why me and her would never be together and she'd never be anything but my baby mama. All she liked to do was party, drink, and smoke. If it wasn't for me, she would be somewhere homeless.

Yeah, I bought her this house a few months after I found out she was having my seed. It was on the West Side, but not in too much of a bad area. They called it Warrendale, and it was borderline Dearborn. The place itself was a nice three bedroom, I fixed it up and let her move in it. I wasn't going to have my daughter living just any kind of way. If it was up to me, my baby would be living with me, but as you can see Krystal is for all the drama and games, so you know that was never going happen.

I walked up and opened the door, and the moment I stepped in, I was greeted with the sight of the whole living room full of all of Krystal's hood rat-ass friends, smoking and drinking. These thot-ass hoes ain't have nothing better to do at four o'clock in the afternoon I see.

"Where my baby at?" I asked Krystal's sister Passion.

I watched as she begrudgingly twisted around to face me, her lip curled up. "She in the back with her mama," Passion replied with her face turned up. I didn't know what her problem was. She always acting like a nigga did something to her funny-looking ass.

Ignoring her, I walked to the back of the house where my daughter's room was and saw her sitting in between Krystal's legs, getting her hair combed. "Daddy, I missed you sooo much!" she yelled as soon as she saw me walk into the room.

I reached down and picked her up into a big hug. "I missed you too, Babygirl!"

"Okay, put her down so I can finish her hair!" Krystal was always mad when my daughter showed me any kind of love. She was obviously jealous of our relationship. No matter what Krystal said or did to turn my baby girl against me, it never worked.

Even when she would not let her call or go with me for weeks, tell her I was too busy for her, all kinds of bullshit, my Babygirl would always say, "No, my daddy loves me, and I always come first!" I had been teaching her that since she was born.

I put her down so Krystal could do whatever she called what it was she was doing to her hair. After I took her to the mall, I was going to bring her to Brazil to get her hair braided anyway. Krystal was rolling her eyes at me the whole time I was standing there. I knew she was bitter about seeing me and Brittany out the other day, but hey, Brittany was my girl, and I was going to try to start doing right by her.

I was head-over-heels in love with Brittany. She always had a nigga's back when I needed her to, and she was a bread-winner **too**. Now, don't get me wrong, I had enough money to take care of her for the rest of her life, but she wanted to make her own money.

Her dream was to open a dance studio. I offered to buy her a building, but she wanted to do it all on her own. Shit with us has been rough, we had been on and off for years now. I even had a baby while I was dating her and everything, and we still managed to keep it together for the most part.

As soon as Krystal was done, I grabbed my Babygirl and we were on our way out the door. "Zay, we need to talk when you get a chance," she grabbed my arm and told me in a low tone.

"About what, Kris? I'm not for your games today."

Her lip curled up just like her sister's had. "You always got a problem when I want to talk. That's okay. I bet if I was Brittany you wouldn't have turned your face up."

Krystal's ass was always getting smart and bringing my girl up, that's why we only got along when we were fucking. I hated that shit. I really just wanted to co-parent with her. "Why don't you come back tonight, Zay? Come spend the night with me," she offered in her little sexy whining tone.

"Man... Kris, I'm not about to go through this with you today. How I'mma spend the night with you when I got my baby girl?" I was getting annoyed with her ass.

Her arms folded over her chest, hip jutting out. "Leave her with your bitch, I know that's where you 'bout to take her anyway." See what I mean? She was always on some dumb shit. What made her even think that was a good idea to bring up out loud? Dumb shit.

I didn't even say anything, I just grabbed my Babygirl and walked out the door. I wasn't about to be going back and forth about that shit. After shutting the door behind us, I strapped Demi into her car seat and got in.

"Babygirl, where to first, Princess?" I looked back at her, smiling so big it made my face hurt, I loved this little girl so much. She was gorgeous. Her light brown skin was so smooth and creamy, and she had curly brown hair with two dimples that went deeper when she smiled. Spending time with her was the best part of my life, I swear you never knew love until you have a child that loved you no matter what.

"I want to go shopping, Daddy! Pweease!"

"Okay, Babygirl, anything you want."

■■

Rain on me,

Lord, won't you take this pain from me

I don't want to live, I don't want to breathe

Baby just rain on me

—Ashanti

CHAPTER 18

Bianca

It had been about three weeks since I they told me I couldn't get an abortion. I was now eighteen weeks pregnant. I **had been calling my mama every day since The day they said I couldn't get it. I need her to get her to meet me at the clinic again so I could take care of this before it was to late . I have still have not been able to get in touch with her I** couldn't believe I was going through this. Well—I guess I could believe it, I wasn't playing things smart at the time, but I couldn't understand for the life of me why God was putting me through all this.

I mean, yeah, I was wild and fucking around like a thot, but I was young and wanted to have fun. I got all as on every report card every year I was in school, I listened to my sisters for the most part, and I was the captain of the cheer squad and the debate team. I just couldn't understand why karma was kicking me in the ass like this.

I picked up my phone and saw that Marcus had been blowing it up while I was away trying to get my shit together. He had been calling me for days. Hell, all my friends have. I wasn't talking to anyone but Carlos.

I felt a little better now that I had finally told my sisters what was going on, even though we hadn't talked about it since the other day at lunch. Unfortunately, I knew they would be asking me what I was going to do in a few days. They were just trying to give me space, but undoubtedly wondering what I was going to do next. I was wondering the same thing; I was all over the place. One day I was crying and upset, the next I was laughing and joking. I was sick all morning and up all night.

I walked downstairs and caught sight of my sisters in the living room. Zil was reading a book like always, while Britt was watching Green Leaf. "Hey, y'all," I sullenly greeted as I padded over to the couch, sitting next to Britt.

Zil looked up from her book and spoke to me first, her eyes shifting over to me. "What's up, Bebe?"

"Hey, little sis," Brittany said without breaking eye-contact with the TV.

Brazil put her novel down on the coffee table in front of her. "How you feeling, Bianca? Have you thought about what you going to do?"

I knew this was coming. I wasn't ready to even talk about. "Brazil please not right now" I stood up and looked at Brittany to see if she was going to say anything, hoping she wouldn't.

"Well? When, Bianca? When your water break?"

My head dropped at the question. I wasn't even sure myself. "Damn, Zil! Chill out," Brittany cut in before I could answer her.

"Listen, I don't know what I'm going to do, I'm confused and scared!" I burst into tears. I was having a good day and was just trying to kick back with my sisters, I should've known that they were going to ruin it. After all, here was their sixteen-year-old sister, pregnant.

Brittany grabbed me in for a hug. "Aww, Bebe, don't cry! We going figure it out." She let me sob in her arms. Brazil just picked up her book and continue to read. It really hurt that Zil was acting this way toward me, but who could blame her? She had tried her hardest to make sure I was on the straight and narrow. Now look at me, sitting up here, pregnant at sixteen.

"Listen, Bebe, I know you scared, but you don't have that much time to think about it," Brittany explained as she rubbed my back. "Whatever you decide to do, you know me and Zil are going be here to help!"

Once she said that, I looked over to see what Brazil's face looked like, and she didn't change her expression at all. She had a Resting Bitch Face for sure; she didn't even look up from reading. Instead, she continued to read and showed no feelings about what me and Brittany were talking about.

After I got myself together, I went into my room to text Carlos. I already knew he was worried about me, since I hadn't talked to him in a while. He had been calling me over thirteen times just today. I hoped everything was okay.

Carlos answered on the first ring, yelling "BEBE! What the fuck?!"

I blinked. Me and him were always pretty relaxed and laid-back, I almost never heard him this worked up. "What's wrong, Los? I was sleeping, I wasn't feeling good," I explained, without even knowing why I was feeling guilty yet.

"Marcus, it's Marcus! He was shot last night!" he cried all in one breath.

His words echoed in my head. My mouth dropped open in horror. "Oh my God. *Oh my God,* no. *Noooo!"* I felt my voice crack into a shriek. Carlos was still talking, but I wasn't listening to a thing he was saying. I was in a daze; this was the last thing I want to deal with right now.

I had to get to the hospital. "Los, please come get me! I have to see him! Is he okay?" I was babbling now. "Please tell me he's okay... What happened?!"

"Bebe, you want to try listening to me? I just said he's in surgery. This is his second one since it happened. He lost a lot of blood, the bullet hit a main artery, and his lung was punctured. They are trying to repair the main artery now," he rattled off, and this time I could take some of it in.

I was in shock—sick to my stomach, in fact. I love Marcus. Sure, I fucked around with other niggas, but Marcus was my first everything. I *couldn't* lose him. It was like my life was falling apart right before my eyes. I was only sixteen; I shouldn't be going through this, I should be worried about what college I was going to. Not about if my boyfriend was going to die, or what I was going to do about a baby that I wasn't even sure if it was his baby. I was all over the place.

"Bebe, are you still there?"

"Yes, I am," I blurted. "Are you coming?"

I was already throwing on clothes before I got an answer, holding the phone against my cheek with the ball of my shoulder. "Yep, get dressed, I'm on my way," he responded.

We hung up the phone and I hurried and finished hopping into some black leggings and one of Marcus' Jordan hoodies. I was starting to show a little, and I didn't need anyone asking me any questions. God, *please let him be okay!*

■■■

Still thuggin', I ain't let it change me

Realizin' rappers cool with bein' broke long as they famous

Meech told me I'm the greatest way before I signed a major

I wonder how my life would be, I ain't take that Jamaican

You get a chance to kill me, take it, miss, go meet your maker

—EST Gee

CHAPTER 19

KWAME

I was at one of the new spots we were about to open soon. I was getting everything set up, making sure all the stash spots where lowkey. I had installed a false floor where we would keep all the money, and the basement had a secret tunnel that went from this house to another house that was about four blocks away.

I had remodeled this whole house by myself. Yeah, that's right, your boy was good with his hands. I ran a small construction company where I would buy old houses around the city and surrounding areas, remodel them and then sell them for more than six times the price I paid for it—labor included.

I didn't make this trap look like the others we ran; it had to fit in with the other houses on the block. I made the inside look nice as fuck, but the outside was basic as hell. I had about six more houses to do, then we could get operations back up and running. We had been shut down for about two weeks, and it was time for our boy to get back to work.

Plus, we had a shipment coming in soon. Zay was in Mexico with Javier having a meeting with the plug. I sat this one out. I'd much rather stay home and keep shit flowing back here.

I grabbed my phone and checked to see if I had a text from Brazil. She had been heavy on my brain since we stayed the night together. I never really tripped on a girl, but there was something about her that made me click with her. I found myself texting her good morning every day, and we messaged each other on and off all day. She really had a nigga opening.

I was waiting on her to reply with what she wanted to eat for lunch. She had been working all morning, and I was looking forward to grabbing my boo something to eat and bringing it to the shop. I didn't know what me and Brazil would call what we were doing, but I was liking it.

ZIL BAE: Can you get me a sandwich from Louis Deli, I want a corn beef on rye bread with light mustard, 2 pickles, a bag of plain Lays, 2 Kit Kats and a large Pepsi with lite ice

Me: Damn Girl, you don't need all that lol

ZIL BAE: Yesss I DO Im Starving Kwame.

Me: Lol okay Ma, I was just talking shit, I got you. Be there soon

ZIL BAE: Okay I can't wait to see
you and to get my food LOL!!

I was smiling hard as hell at Brazil saying she wanted to see me. I couldn't believe it, I was really falling for her. I had been liking Zil for years, but now that we were getting close, I was really feeling her.

I picked up Zil's food and wheeled my ride into the driveway before hopping out and grabbing the food. When I walked in, Brazil was standing at the booth, taking a picture of a wig she had just installed. Zil was really good at this hair shit.

When she spun the chair around and I saw whose hair she was doing, I almost dropped her food. Sitting in her chair was my ex-girl Mya. Then again, she wasn't really my girl, but me and her kicked it for about a year. I left her ass alone because she was trying to lock a nigga down, always talking about having a baby and getting married.

I walked in on her on the phone with her homegirl one time telling her how she was poking holes in the condoms tonight. I threw that rat-ass bitch out of my house. I couldn't believe her ass. I ain't seen her since that shit went down.

She looked me dead in the face and grinned. "Oh, hey Kwame, long time no see."

"Yeah." I was being short with her ass. I didn't have time to get into all that with her trifling self in front of Brazil, and I knew she was just trying to make me look bad.

She tried to laugh casually, but I could tell she cared more than she was letting on. "Damn, for real, it's like that?

I ain't think it was no beef." Mya stood up and looked in the mirror.

I laughed at her right back and turned to pull Brazil in for a hug. "It's not no beef. I mean, what you want me to say?" Moving my attention to Zil, my smile became a lot more genuine. "Hey Baby," I greeted as I kissed Brazil on the cheek.

As soon as I did that Mya tuned her face up. "Oh, that's why you acting all funny, 'cause Zil's your girl now," she snorted.

Mya was trying to be messy, and I was about to shut that shit down real fast. Brazil wasn't my girl, but I wasn't about to let this girl do the most like we had something still going on. "Mya, please don't even try to pull no mess in here, okay?" I turned and looked at Brazil. She was just standing there watching me and Mya while drinking her Pepsi.

My ex smirked, hardly even trying to play dumb anymore. "I ain't trying to pull no mess, I'm just saying you one-word-answering me like we wasn't together for a year." Mya was really pulling this shit today. I should've known she was going be on some bullshit soon as she seen me.

I shut her down really fast. "Mya, come on now, man," I groaned at her antics. "You know we wasn't together. The only reason you trying to cut up is 'cause I came up here to bring my baby some food, some shit I never done for you, and you feel a way about it. Maybe if you wasn't on no hood rat thot shit then this could've been you." She was just standing there with her face frowned up, looking crazy.

I turned my attention back to Brazil. "Baby, finish up with her, I'mma set your food up so you can eat in the back,"

I told her, mostly so I had an excuse to leave. I grabbed the bag of food and walked to the back of the shop where the breakroom was.

I was really feeling Brazil, and I wasn't about to just stand there and keep going back and forth with a bitch I wasn't even thinking about. Shit was mad disrespectful. I knew how Mya could get and I wasn't even about to go there with her. I hope Brazil wasn't feeling rubbed the wrong way about what happened.

About fifteen minutes later, Brazil walked into the room to join me. She didn't look like she had a problem, but she was hard to read, so I just waited to see what she was going to say. "Damn, Kwame, I ain't know you used to fuck with Mya," she noted to me as she took a bite of her sandwich

"Man, Baby, that was a year ago," I dismissed. "I ain't seen that girl since I put her out my house for telling her friend she was poking holes in the condoms." I couldn't believe I was explaining myself to her, but I liked the friendship we had, and I wasn't trying to fuck it up just because a rat bitch was in her feelings.

She waved the free hand that wasn't holding her sandwich. "It's okay, I ain't tripping, Kwame, I was just curious. I am not mad at all, I know what kind of bitch she is. Now she gonna keep coming around just to see what I got going on."

I chuckled. "I'm glad that you are hip, Baby, I really like this little thing that we have going on."

She giggled in response, taking a swig of her drink. "And what is this so-called 'little thing' we have going on?"

I didn't even know what to call this 'thing' but I liked it, and I had to be quick with my answers.

"It's called 'HOMIE LOVER'," I said with a smile.

"I like that..." Brazil admitted with a cheek full of food.

I sat with Brazil while she ate her lunch, and we kicked it, laughing and talking about everything we could think of. I think 'HOMIE LOVER' was the perfect name for what we had going on. I mean, after all, we were homies, and we did a few things that lovers do.

As bad as I didn't want to leave my baby, I had to get back to work. I had a few more things to take care of before we opened back up. I kissed Brazil on the cheek and dipped. Damn I can't believe Baby had me opened up like this.

Tied into the game, it ain't no way out

If I go back broke, then I'ma run it up again

Murder that she wrote and then I went and took the pen

—No Cap

CHAPTER 20

♥Brittany♥

I couldn't believe my little sister was pregnant. Okay, fine, I guess I can believe it. She was so hot in the ass, and I might be the one to blame for that. I tried not to be as hard on her as Brazil, but now I guess I should've been. Then our weak-ass Mama was pulled that stunt. I know Bebe was going through it.

Me and Brazil tried our best to keep her away from her so that she wouldn't be disappointed like we were. Mama had done so much hoe shit to us; I don't know why Bianca didn't expect that. But, I guess she had to see for herself.

Brazil was in a good head space at least, and I was really feeling that. I was happy she wasn't in her feelings about Ron's lame-ass. I wondered about Zil a lot—she always was the strongest out of us. She was so unbothered. I get that she was into the spiritual-ass positive vibe shit, but everyone has a breaking point.

I never, not one time, saw Zil reach hers. Sure, she gets mad and shuts down. But a breaking point? Naw, I've never seen my sister reach hers yet. She had been kicking it with Kwame lately, which was a surprise to me.

She always acted like she didn't like Kwame before, but he was keeping a smile on her face. I didn't know what they called whatever they were doing, but I'm here for it if it made her happy. Besides, Kwame was a good guy. Now yeah, he was in the streets, but you never heard about Kwame having girl problems at all.

To think about it, I never saw him take interest in a woman fully. I had been with Zay for years and still, Kwame was single and had been the whole time I knew him. He had hoes he fucked with from time to time, but a girlfriend. Not yet. So, if my sister was going give any hood nigga a chance, I'm glad that it would be him.

I walked downstairs to the kitchen and Brazil was cleaning up. She had her sage burning and her music playing over her speaker. "Hey, B," Zil greeted while wiping down the stove.

"What's up, Sister?" I replied as I grabbed a bowl to make me some cereal.

She tossed the rag she was using into the sink, then started washing her hands. "Nothing much, just straightening up a little bit so I can meet Kwame downtown. I'm going with him to look at a building he wants to get to expand his construction company," she explained.

"Okay, okay, Zil," I snickered, grabbing my spoon. "I see you and Kwame been hanging out a lot lately, huh?" I asked after swallowing, since I had a mouth full of Corn Pops.

Her lips pursed. "Yeah, that my homie-lover friend." Brazil blushed soon as she said that.

"Lover?" I repeated. "Oh, y'all lovers now?"

Her shoulders lifted and then dropped in a bashful shrug, an attempt to brush me off her trail. "Not really *lovers* but, you know..." I had seen Brazil with Ron for years, but when I tell you I had never seen my sister's face light up so much just from saying someone name, I wasn't joking. It was weird, but also cute at the same time.

I was happy she was in a good head space. I know I was always doing my own thing, but I really cared about my little sisters, I just also tried to let them live their own lives. Speaking of living their life, I haven't really heard much from Bianca, or seen her for that matter. I knew she was still pregnant. I wondered what she was going to do.

I really didn't want my baby sister to have a baby, but I would support her and help her as much as I can. We needed to sit to down and really have a talk with her; get a plan in motion. "Zil, you talked to Bebe? I been texting her, but no response."

"Nope, not today," she admitted. "I texted her last night, but she didn't respond. I looked in her room, and she wasn't there. I'm really worried 'bout her, B," Zil sighed with a sad look in her eye.

I rubbed the back of my neck. "I am too, but I was trying to give her some space to figure everything out. Y'know, neither one of us have been through what she's going through, but we really need to sit her down and have a heart to heart."

"You're right," she agreed. "I'll try to get in touch with her and plan something for tonight." Zil then picked up her phone and began to scroll Facebook.

I was looking in my phone as well, texting Passion. She was begging me to come over, and I had been ignoring her ass. Passion wasn't happy with fucking around every now and then—she wanted to be in a full-blown relationship with me, which would never work.

First and foremost, like I said before, I didn't want a girlfriend. I messed with girls every now and then, but I could never see myself leaving dick alone completely. Secondly, Passion was Krystal's sister, and I was done being messy.

Don't get me wrong, when me and Passion were together, we vibed good as hell. But that all it was: a vibe. I wasn't in love with her. Maybe what I was feeling was lust. Whatever the case, I just wanted to have fun from time to time. I left Passion on read. I knew that was going to start some mess later, but I just didn't feel like dealing with her right now.

Then, there was Zay. He had been calling and texting me all morning too. I wasn't really mad at him; I was just over all this *drama* he had going on. It seemed like every time we were doing good, he did something to piss me off—or his rat-ass baby mama came around causing problems.

She was always putting on a show. I knew it was because Zay was still fucking her. I know what you're thinking: I should just leave him alone, get some one that's all for me. Sure, I've tried, but you can't tell me you haven't been in love with someone and been under their spell. It's like Zay had his fingers wrapped around my heart.

I knew he was no good for me anymore. Back when we were young it was cool, but now I was older and wiser. I deserve my own man who was down for me and only me. I had big plans; I wanted to move to LA and open a dance school, and I was almost to my goal.

That wasn't to say that I didn't have money, but I wanted to be able to take my sisters with me and not have to worry about anything. I wanted to help Zil get her own shop and start her line of haircare products. I had plans for us; I was just caught up in this Detroit lifestyle. If you ever lived in Detroit, then you know what I mean.

"Oh my God!"

The cry snapped me out of my thoughts. "What's wrong, Zil?!" I demanded as I jumped up and ran into the living room to see what was wrong.

"Bebe just posted on Facebook! 'Praying for my man, I know God got you' and she tagged that she was at Henry Ford Hospital" Zil handed me her phone so I could see her post.

I scrolled through the comments and learned that Marcus had been shot and was in the middle of his third surgery. I felt so bad for my sister. Not only was she pregnant, but her baby daddy was fighting for his life. Damn, Bebe, this is not the life of a sixteen-year-old.

She should've been hanging around with her friends, planning summer trips, shopping, and going on college tours, but instead she was pregnant, dealing with our dead-beat mother, and her boyfriend was in the hospital. I had to hurry and get dressed to be with her, so I rushed upstairs to shower; I needed to go see about my baby.

I had just stepped out the shower and, my phone was ringing—it was Passion again. I let it ring and sent her to the voicemail message. Refocusing, I oiled my body with coconut oil, and put on a pair of black biker shorts with a black and red sports bra from Nike to match. I threw on a cherry-colored T-shirt on top, slipped on my red and black Nike Runners, and pulled my naturally curly hair up into a messy bun. I made a mental note to have Zil Sew my bundles back in.

By the time I finished getting myself together, Passion had called me ten times. I would be adding this shit on top of everything she had done wrong, and as soon as I was done checking on my sister, I'd confront her.

It took no time for me and Brazil to reach Henry Ford Main. Soon as we walked in the doors, I saw Bebe, all balled up in the corner in a chair, sleeping. Marcus family was all there too, filling up the rest of the chairs.

I tapped Bianca lightly on her arm, and she jumped up, her eyes wide. "Hey B, hey Zil." The moment our names left her mouth, she burst into tears. Zil wrapped her arms and rocked our sister as she cried her heart out. After about ten minutes, Bebe got herself together and recomposed herself.

I sat down next to her and asked, "So, what happen Bebe? Is he going to be okay?"

"We don't know; he's still in surgery," Bianca answered.

Zil bit her lip. "What happened? Did anyone say?"

Our younger sister went quiet, staring down at her clasped hands, fingers messily laced together. "Los said that some niggas from the other side shot up one of the spots that Marcus work at. Him and two other people got hit—" Bebe's voice cracked, and she started crying again. "I haven't really been talking to him like that with everything that's going on. I feel so bad... If I would've been texting him back, this might not have happened."

Brazil chimed in with, "Bianca, don't you dare blame yourself for this. We all know what comes from messing with hood niggas."

Our younger sister finally cracked a smile at her words, confused. "Aww, Zil, please don't start. You wouldn't know nothing about messing with no hood nigga."

"Yes, she do; she been messing with Kwame," I laughed.

"Oooh, bitch, and you ain't tell me?!" Bebe was smiling from ear to ear. "I want all the tea!" As y'all know, Zil was the good girl out of all of us, so this was probably a shocker for her.

Brazil blushed, looking away. "Ain't no tea, we just cool. We just been chilling and vibing, no big deal," she insisted, brushing Bianca off.

I rolled my eyes at *that* fib. "Oh, it's a big deal," I disagreed with a smirk on my face. "He been over almost every night since we went out." Me and my sister talked and laughed for a while after that. Despite everything that was going on, we got to catch up and kick it without arguing. For us to live in the same house, we really haven't seen or heard from each other that much.

After about an hour a doctor came out into the lobby, looking over at our group. "Family of Lamarcus Matthews?"

Bebe stood up and walked up to the doctor with his mom and little brother, while his friends that were there stayed in the background with me and Brazil. We could still hear what the doctor was saying. "Mr. Matthews is a very lucky young man, me and my team worked very long and hard to save his life," the older man explained. "He lost a lot of blood, and we had to repair both is lungs. We put him into a medically induced coma to give his body time to rest. You can see him now, two people at a time."

I was so glad that Marcus was going to be okay. Lord knows Bianca didn't need to go through anything else. Bianca let his mom and brother go in and see him first, while she came and sat down next to us, waiting to go back.

I looked at the clock. It was now almost five PM, so I needed to go home and get ready for work. Tonight, was my stage show with Passion. I really didn't feel like her drama tonight, but this my biggest night of the week, so I had to play it cool until after the show, which would be when I was breaking it off with her. I might even chill on dancing for a while. I really needed to spend more time with my sisters and help Bebe get her mind right.

We left the hospital after Bebe sat with Marcus an hour or so. She was a train wreck. She cried the whole time we were in the car. Then when we got home, she went up into her room and cried some more. I felt terrible for my baby.

She shouldn't be going through so much pain at such a young age. She should be getting in trouble for staying out too late, not worrying about if she was going to keep her baby and if the father was going to live.

My phone was ringing off the hook soon as I turned it on. I had turned it off while I was at the hospital, and after skimming over my notifications, I noticed I had missed a ton of texts from Passion and Zay. As I read the messages, my annoyance with Passion was climbing. She was crazy as hell. You could tell that her and Krystal were sisters.

My phone rang again, and it was Zay calling. "Hey, what's going on? Where are you, I been calling you all day!" Zay barked as soon as I picked up the call, sounding irritated.

His tone made me raise my eyebrows. "I was at the hospital with Bianca. Her boyfriend got shot last night," I answered flatly, wondering to myself why was I explaining myself to him.

"Yeah, I know, B, that's what I was calling you for!" His tone was wearing me out. "Marcus was shot at one of my houses. I don't know who's doing this or what is going on, but I need to get to the bottom of this quick, B. I been in the game for a while now, I don't have beef. How could I when everyone in the D work for me?"

I shook my head. There was way too much going on right now, it was overwhelming. "Damn, Zay I didn't know that was your house. Now what are you going to do?" I asked him, because I remembered he had just opened back up a few of his houses after he got hit, and I knew the police would be watching them a lot more closely now.

His groan filled the speaker. "Man, B, I don't know!" He sounded like he was at his wit's end. "I'mma have to shut down again till I find out who behind all this shit. I'm supposed to be going to see my people in a few days, I thought I was going have everything under control before I went to see them, too." Zay breathed in, then sighed it out. Despite how tired of his baby mama foolishness, it tugged at my heart. "I hate to have to tell him I don't have my shit under control."

I could tell that Zay was going through it. He said he would come to see me at the club later, and I knew he was upset, because he never came to see me while I was dancing. He usually would wait to see me after work, but when he was going through something and I had one of my shifts, he would come up there, get the biggest booth, and pay for me to dance for him all night.

He had never been there on the night I had to do a stage show, though. This was going to a night to remember. I had to figure out how I was going to pull this off, and fast. Passion was going be all over me, and she was going to expect me to leave with her like we always did. I wasn't going to be able to do that with Zay there. I might could call off, but this was one of my biggest nights of the week. I was stuck between a rock and a hard place.

The Risks We Take for Love

So you fuckin' with a real one

Now you fuckin' with a real one

Somebody should have told you

I wanna fuck with you

—Party Next Door

CHAPTER 21

I was really in a good space in my life. I mean my sisters were going through a lot, but me personally? I was good. My little sister was dealing with the worst of it. I must admit I was pissed when she told me she was pregnant, but I have washed my hands with trying to run her life. Yes, I love my sister to death, but I learned that being hard on her wasn't going to stop her from doing what she wanted to do.

Me and Kwame were kicking it every day. I still didn't know what to call what we doing other than by the name we had come up with, but it was cool. I didn't think that me and him would vibe like we did. He wasn't really my type—well, I thought he wasn't anyway. He was something different, though.

Kwame was a street nigga, and I had always tried my best to stay away from them. I saw on many occasions what Zay did to my sister, and I always said I wasn't going to be putting myself through stuff like that. I ended up going through it anyway.

Ron worked a nine to five, was in law school, and came from a two-parent household. I thought he was different from the guys Britt had dated, and that it really wouldn't be difficult for him to be with me and only me, but I guess I was wrong. He was just as bad as any other nigga, just look at how he cheated on me more than once.

I guess you couldn't judge a book by it cover. To be honest, I didn't have a mother around to teach me about dating, I just listened to my sister cry more than enough when were young to know I didn't want to go through half the stuff she went through. That's why I was so hard on Bianca. I didn't want to ever see my little sister experience that shit.

I had just finished up at the shop and was waiting on Kwame to pick me up. He had dropped me off after we went to lunch because I had to do two ponytails. We had planned on spending the day together, but the two girls who called were some of my regulars, so I decided to take their appointment. Plus, Kwame had to make a run, so it all worked out perfectly.

About ten minutes after I texted him and told him I was ready, he was walking in the shop with two dozen white roses. I was smiling from ear to ear, and my dark creamy brown skin had turned red from blushing. "Oh my God, Kwame!" I squealed as I ran up to him and wrapped my arms around his neck.

"You ready, Baby?" he asked as he smooched me on my forehead.

I couldn't stop smiling. "Yes, I'm ready. Man, these are so pretty; white roses are my favorite!" Kwame had kept me smiling a lot now days. When I was with him, I forgot about everything going on. I was so worried about my little sister having a baby, or how every other day how I heard Brittany and Zay fighting. As y'all might be aware, I was like the mother of the family. I worried so much about them, and it was nice to let my mind rest easy for a little bit.

"Where we going, Kwame? You passed my house," I pointed out as we rode past my exit.

"You'll see when we get there." He had a big Kool-Aid smile, showing off his pretty white teeth. I had retwisted his dreads a few days ago, and today, he wore them up in a messy bun. His green eyes sparkled every time the sun hit them. Lord, he was so fine, I found myself just staring at him sometimes.

Where he was taking me? He had already brought me to breakfast this morning, and after that, we went to look at a few buildings for sale to see if I wanted one of them for the shop, I planned on opening up soon. After the third property, that's when I got the call to go do hair. He picked me up with two-dozen roses and now he was taking me somewhere way past the hood. We were now close to Monroe. With all that in mind, I wracked my brain to try to figure out his plan.

For the last two weeks, he had made sure to do something nice for me. It was a nice change of pace after Ron, who only ever seemed to do anything sweet in an attempt to get into my pants. Me and Kwame, on the other hand, hadn't tried anything sexually since that night at the club. He knew I was a virgin, and he also knew I was drunk that night and that we had gone too far. I didn't regret it, but I also don't think I want to go any further just yet. I was in rare form that night and in my feelings—that's the real reason I even let thing go that far.

We pulled up to a wraparound driveway with a huge house at the end of it. I had never seen a home so big—other than on TV. He stopped the car and turned it off. "Come on, Baby, let's go," he urged, looking at me with the same smile he wore the whole ride.

"Whose house is this, Kwame?"

"It's ours for the next few days," he responded. "I know you been going through some shit with your sisters, so I just want you to relax and let all that go for a little while. Come on."

We got out of the car and walked to the two big glass doors, which he unlocked and stepped through, and I followed inside. This place was the most beautiful thing I had ever seen.

It had a spiral staircase just a few feet from the front door, with a white and silver marble floor that was so clear and clean that I was scared to walk on it. The living room sat down to the right of the stairs and was blanketed in a big fluffy white carpet. Inside it was an all-white and gold plush couch and love seat, while over the fireplace was a huge picture of a white and black tiger. When I glanced into the kitchen, it was almost as big as my whole house. I was lost for words.

Up the steps were bedrooms, each one bigger than the next. In the master bedroom sat a California king bed and a small couch off to the side. There was a balcony in the back, and from it, you could see the backyard and pool.

I couldn't believe he had rented this house just for us to spend the night in. We didn't even need all this space! I walked around the house, admiring every room. "I ran you a bath in the master bathroom, so head in there, enjoy a nice bath, relax, read your book, and I'll be up in an hour so we can have dinner. There are clothes in the closet, and everything is brand-new, so wear whatever you want."

I had no words. No one had ever done anything so nice for me before. I had been with Ron for years, and don't get me wrong, he did do things for me, but nothing like this. I walked into the master bathroom, and the tub was big enough for at least three adults to fit inside it comfortably. To boot, Kwame had real rose petals floating in the water, and candles lit around the tub. There was soft music playing, and there was even a bath tray with a glass of champagne and a Kindle on it.

I undressed and stepped in. The water was scorching hot, just how I liked it. I let my body slip down into the water and began to relax. It was so peaceful. All the stuff my sisters was going through came to mind as I slid my eyes shut. I know B was going to be able to handle her own; I was more worried about Bebe. She was so young and going through so much. I took a drink from the glass, grabbed the Kindle, and began to read.

"Brazil. *Brazil.*" I opened my eyes, and Kwame was standing there with a robe. I must have drifted off, because the water was now cold. "I take it you enjoyed your bath?" he asked, smiling.

I smiled right back "Yes, I did," I admitted. This was what I really needed, Kwame, some time to unwind and relax. Thank you so much for this," I said as I stepped out and into the robe he was holding.

He pulled me in for a hug and the smell of Gucci Guilty mixed with weed filled my nose. I felt my heart start beating fast. He kissed me in the nape of my neck, and I let out a soft moan. "Kwame, go'n," I giggling as I pulled away. I had to, because Kwame's touch was making me feel a type of way. I kept telling myself that I wasn't ready to take it there, but every time he touched me, my body was saying something else.

"You know you want me touching and kissing on you," Kwame retorted as he walked out the bathroom.

It was like he was reading my mind. "Boy, hush and pick me something out to throw on so we and have dinner," I bristled bashfully. "What are we having anyway?"

"Hurry up and get dressed so you can see," he encouraged with this silly smile on his face as he walked out the room. I padded into the closet to see what he had picked out for me to wear. Inside, I saw a red lace thong and a matching bra, but that was all. He was crazy if he thought I was going to have dinner in my underwear.

I looked through all the clothes, and there was so many things to pick from. I just couldn't believe that he really rented out this house and brought all these clothes just for me. I decided on some Nike biker shorts and a cropped T-shirt. Before I left, I slipped on a pair of Nike socks and went downstairs.

Kwame was fixing our plates, and I once again marveled at the huge kitchen. He turned and looked at me with his nose turned up. "That is not what I picked for you," he noted.

It didn't sound irritated or demanding, so I just laughed. "I know," I replied with a smile on my face. "I wasn't coming to have dinner in just my underwear!"

Kwame snorted. "Why not? Ain't nobody else here but us, and I done seen it all anyway," he pointed out as he put our plates down on the island.

My brown cheeks turned red just hearing him bring up that night, but I don't know why I was so embarrassed about it. "Boy, hush," I repeated once more. "So, what you cook? Or what did you have someone cook for us?" I joked playfully as I pushed him.

"Girl, I cooked all this food, stop playing," he proudly responded as he poured us a glass of wine. I sat down at the table placed my napkin in my lap.

Kwame had made us ribeye steaks, garlic red skin potatoes, fresh green beans, and shrimp with a white cream sauce. It looked so good, like something from a 5-star restaurant. I cut a piece of the steak, and it was so tender that it melted in my mouth. We ate in silence for a while because I was so lost in how good the food was that I didn't even think to even spark up a conversation.

Kwame read my mind yet again. "Damn, Zil, I take it you liked your food, 'cause you ain't said not one word," he giggled.

"Yesss, it's so good..." I said with a bite of steak tucked into my cheek. I had cleared my whole plate—I was stuffed. Despite that, I helped Kwame clean up the kitchen and put the rest of the food up.

We went in the living room to watch a movie. I was relaxed and in a good headspace. After all, I really enjoyed spending time with him. I felt like I was having an out of body experience, being here—with him. A guy like Kwame.

My thoughts were once more wandering back to Britt and Zay; I couldn't imagine having to deal with that shit. Yeah, Britt had any and everything she needed, plus some more, but you should hear them fighting.

Krystal stayed making statuses and posting Zay on her story. It was just a mess. I that hated my sister had to go through it all. I get that Zay helped us out a lot when our mom first left, but how much was she supposed to take? Zay used that against her every time she tried to leave his ass.

"Zil, what you want to watch?" Kwame asked, pulling me from my thoughts.

"It don't matter. Something funny," I suggested.

"How High, Super Bad, or Stepbrothers?" he asked.

The question made me smile. "Super Bad. That's one of my favorite movies. I'mma pop some popcorn." With that, I got up and walked to the kitchen.

I had left my phone on the island and plugged into the charger because I just wanted to enjoy my time with Kwame and not have to worry about nothing just for a little while. Unfortunately, as soon as I picked up my phone, I noticed that I had around five missed calls and ten texts. Most of the messages were from my clients, but one stood out to me. It was from "Kimberly," which was what I had entered my mom's number as in my caller ID. Now why in the world is she texting me?

KIM: Call me Zilly ASAP

■■■

The Risks We Take for Love

You know if you cared anything about love

You woulda been front and center

Lovin' me and touchin' me

Honey

Honey

You know if you knew anything about me

You woulda been much more tender

—Toni Braxton

CHAPTER 22

I texted all my daughters to call me ASAP. Now, I know y'all may not like me very much, but you people don't know a damn thing about me or my reason for leaving my girls. I'm sure there are plenty of you who think that there isn't anything in the world that would make you leave your kids, but don't judge me until you know the full story.

I couldn't stay and look after them, I had a lot going on in life at the time and leaving them was the best thing for me to do. I had my kids at a young age, after all. Now, don't get things twisted, I loved and cared for them the best I could; they never went without food or clothes. Either way, I never wanted them kids to be honest.

I was with their father, Brian, since high school, and he was my first love. We had gone to prom together, and that's the night I got pregnant with Brittany. I was scared and embarrassed, but Brian reassured that we would be okay.

We were doing good at first. I was going to community college, and he worked at Ford. We had bought our first little house on the west side of Detroit—then I got pregnant again with Brazil. I didn't want to keep her, but Brian and my mother were against me getting an abortion.

I cried myself to sleep every night. Here I was, pregnant again, with only six months away from my degree. I was so sick with Brazil, I dropped out of school, and I was so miserable the whole time, up until the day she was born. My baby girl was so pretty with her brown skin and curly black hair. The thought of not wanting her left my mind the moment I saw her; I couldn't believe I ever had the thought of killing her.

I had been a stay-at-home mom since I had Brazil, and everything was back to normal. I wasn't back in school, and yet, I was content with my life. Me and Brian weren't getting along that much, but I was still content, because I had my girls, and I enjoyed spending all my time with them. I would do a few of my friends' hair during the day, and they would be right there with me.

Brian was staying out later and later; he didn't spend much time with me or the girls. I wasn't tripping, though, because I was sick of him anyway. He didn't want me to do hair, and he only gave me a little bit of money once a week.

It like he changed after Brazil was born. He was so against me having an abortion, but as soon as she was three months, it's like he switched up. He stayed out late, and sometimes, he didn't come home at all. At first, I would bitch about it, but soon, I just stopped caring. I was making my own money and putting it up so I could move out of his house.

I was doing one of my homegirl's hair one day, and she told me she had seen Brian and a girl named Mika checking into the hotel she worked in. I was more embarrassed than I was hurt. I had a feeling he was cheating on me, but I never had any proof of it. I know we weren't married, but we had two daughters and had been together for years. Maybe that's why he never asked me to marry him.

Following that, a few months had gone by since I learned of Brian cheating on me. I played it so cool. I was laying it on thick: cooking, cleaning, and fucking him whenever I had the chance. I had almost enough money to move out, because I was working hard and even taking house calls.

He didn't know I was leaving him soon. I don't even think he cared. The only thing I could think he would be mad about was me taking his kid. He didn't spend much time with them but when he did, that was the happiest I ever saw him. He would give the girls candy and ice cream, get them all hyper, and then leave me to try to calm them down.

One night, me and the girls were lying in bed, watching TV, and of course Brian wasn't home. There was a knock on the door. I told Brittany and Brazil to stay put, threw on my robe, and went to see who could be knocking at this time of night.

I snatched the door open and there stood a little skinny woman holding a baby about a year younger than Brazil. "Kimmy? You might not know me, but I know you. I'm Sue, and this here," She held the little boy out to me "Is Brian Jr."

I felt my chest get tight and my world start spinning. I had to get myself together. I took two deep breaths, and at first, I was going to slap her in her face, but then I thought about it.

She didn't owe me anything. It was Brian who was supposed to be loyal to me, not her. That's where women messed up at, thinking the other woman owes you something. Still, that didn't mean they were entirely blameless. If you know a man has a woman, then why even fuck with him? You know the chance that he will leave her for you is impossibly small.

The scrawny woman had her son in her arms, and with how hard it was raining, there had to be a good reason she was here. I invited her in. "Come in. Let's talk."

About two hours later, she had given me the rundown on her and Brian's whole relationship. She told me that she hadn't heard from him in about three months. He had stopped paying her rent, and she was about to get put out. She came over here, not to start anything, but to try to find him before her and his only son were put out on the streets.

I knew Brian was cheating on me, but damn, to have another child, whew, it was the icing on the cake. I didn't know what Sue wanted from me. I mean, I could call him for her, but that was about it. I didn't have any money to give.

She asked if I would, and I told her that nine times out of ten, he wouldn't answer but I'd give it a try. I dialed his number, and it went straight to voice mail. Normally I would only call him once, but I dialed it again and it began to ring.

"Hello?"

"Hello Brian, where are you?" I asked, trying to sound as normal as I could.

"I'm out, Kim. What's up? Everything good?"

I rolled my eyes at his response. What did he mean he was out? Obviously. It was damn near two AM. "Well, I think you need to come home. Someone is here to see you."

He gave a mean-spirited scoff. "To see me? Who could be there to see me at this time of night, Kim? I don't have time for your games, I'll be home when I get there!"

He hung up in my face. That was just like him, to cut the conversation short. I let Sue know that he hung up and wasn't coming home anytime soon and told her she could stay here until he came.

I knew that when he got home, he would be so mad when he saw Sue and his son here, but I didn't care. This was going to be me and my girls' last night here. I didn't have enough money to move in my own spot, but I was going back home to my mother's house. I would continue to do hair until I was able to get my own place.

The next morning, I woke up to see Sue and Brian Jr. still asleep on the couch. Instead of waking them up, I went into the kitchen and started breakfast. The girls would be up soon, and I had to make sure they ate, and all our stuff was packed before Brian came home. He would probably be here soon, because he had to be at work today and his work clothes were here. I didn't know *what* Sue was going to do, but I was leaving today, whether he came home or not.

It was about ten AM now and I had all me and the girls' stuff loaded in the car. Sue was putting Brian Jr. in his car seat and was getting ready to go home. I told her I would be in touch with her so that we could keep the kids close no matter what Brian said, and we said our goodbyes.

As soon as we were pulling off Brian was pulling up. When Sue saw him, she jumped out of the car and went crazy. She was screaming and yelling about how he played her. How he begged her to keep this baby and now he was singing a whole different tune.

I sat in my car and listened to the whole thing. At first, I was about to pull off, but I just sat and took it all in. Brian then walked up to my car, and I hit the locks. He banged on the window, yelling, "And where the fuck you think you going?"

"I am leaving, Brian," I told him through the window. "I'm so over you and all the cheating. I can tell you haven't been happy in a while, plus you got a lot going on, as you can see," I explained, said pointing to Sue as she was putting Brian Jr into Brian's car.

He ran over to her and soon as it was clear I was done, I pulled off. I was over all of this. Me and my girls were going to be just fine without him.

After getting settled in my old room, I went down the stairs to talk to my mom. There wasn't much to explain, because she knew everything that was going on between Brian and me. My mom was like my best friend, so we talked about everything, and she told me to leave Brian a long time ago. I was scared of what people would think of me having to come back home. I should've listened to my mom.

I had been sick for the last week. Whatever stomach bug I had, I couldn't shake it. I was lucky to be at my mom's house, because I couldn't even get out of bed. Thankfully, she was a big help with the girls. I had only heard from Brian maybe twice since we been here, and it had been almost a month. He never called about the girls it was always asking about when I would be coming back, or if I had stopped acting crazy yet.

I couldn't take being sick any longer, so I went to Henry Ford Hospital to get checked out. I waited in the ER for about an hour in a half when a nurse called my name for me to come to the back. "Kimberly Blackwell? Here." She passed me a plastic container. "I'm going to need you to pee in this cup. When you are done, get undressed and the doctor will be right in."

Once I finished, I sat and waited for the doctor to come in. I had a feeling what he was going to tell me. About forty-five minutes later, he came in.

"Ms. Blackwell, how are you today?" he asked.

I shrugged. "I'm doing okay. I haven't been feeling well," I explained, trying to hold back the constant urge to throw up.

"I see congrats are in order." He gave a big smile, and I felt my stomach flip even harder. "You are pregnant. We will get you up to ultrasound so we can see how far along you are."

My mind was racing. I was pregnant again? I couldn't have another baby! Me and Brian were over, and I wasn't in any position to have another kid. I knew my mother wouldn't support me if I were to have an abortion. I was lost and confused; I had no clue what to do next.

I had no choice but to tell my mother I was having another baby. I knew she would be behind me a hundred percent of the way. However, I didn't know how I was going tell Brian. Maybe I wouldn't tell him.

I had been calling all my kids all day, and none of them were answering. I don't know why I expected them to. I was still their mother at the end of the day, the woman that left them. Brittany *hated* me. She was old enough to see everything that I went through when things went bad, but not old enough to understand it.

I need them to help me. I know you're probably wondering why they would help me after I let them down time and time again. Not that I had an answer. I was behind on the rent, and I didn't have any food in my house. I haven't heard from Jake in a while, and there wasn't any telling where he was.

I was supposed to use the money I got from Bianca to pay my bills, but the day she gave me the cash, I went to the bar and ran into my old trick and a few friends. We got high and partied for the rest of the week. Now I'm sitting here looking crazy. Once the high goes down and the partying is over, I was back to my real life. I didn't have anything without Jake. Sometimes, I wished I didn't leave my girls back then. But hey, you can't change the past.

I'm young but I'm wise

Enough to know that you

Don't fall in love over night

That's why I thought if I

Took my time that everything

In love would be right

But as soon as I closed my eyes

I was saying to love "Goodbye."

–-Brandy

CHAPTER 23

I had been at the hospital every day with Marcus since he got out of surgery. It had been a month, and he still hadn't woken up yet. The doctors said I should give him some time, that he had been through a lot and his body is resting. I had faith that he would be okay.

I couldn't wait for him to wake up, I was so stressed out about everything that was going on. I was still pregnant and had to face the fact that I was really having a baby. I couldn't wait to tell Marcus that we would be having a daughter. I found out it was a girl about a week ago. Although I didn't know if it was Marcus' baby, I was never going to tell anyone that . I couldn't, and plus the other guy , he wanted me to get an abortion, so it wasn't like he was going to come looking for me or the baby anyway. I had blocked him on everything.

My mama had been reaching out to me and my sisters, but none of us were answering. She should've known that Britt and Zil weren't going to talk to her. I kind of wanted to, even though she played me and ran off with my money. **Now she need something from me and wants to reach out . It was too late now to get an abortion so I really didn't**

have nothing to say to her . I really I wanted a relationship with her. My sisters hated her so much, but I was so young when she left; I didn't understand, and when I was old enough to understand, it really didn't bother me that much. **But after how she went M.I.A on me I really had a lot to reconsider.**

I sat there and read my book while holding Marcus' hand. When I felt him squeeze my hand, I thought I was tripping. I looked up from my book and his eyes where open. "Bebe Bae. Hey," he greeted with a voice that was very low and dry

"Don't try to talk. Let me get you some water, Baby." I got up and grabbed my water bottle off the table, then put the water to his lips and watched as he took a small drink.

He then spoke again. "How long I been out?" he asked, now sounding like himself, but still talking very quietly. It was hard to hear him.

"About a month," I briskly answered. "Hold on, Baby, let me get the doctor. I'll fill you in on everything that's been going on."

After the doctor came qin and checked on Marcus, he told us that he should make a full recovery. That was *so* good to hear. I let Marcus call his mom and let her know that he was awake. Her and his family were already on their way down here, so it worked out great. I decided to tell him about the baby before everyone arrived and crowded up the place. "So, Marcus. I got something to tell you..."

His brow scrunched up. "What's up, Bebe?"

"Well... I'm pregnant with you daughter..." I admitted.

Marcus' eyes almost popped out of his head. "Stop playing, Bianca," he urged. I wasn't sure if he was pale because he was horrified, or because he had just woken up from a month-long coma.

"I'm for real." I pulled up my hoodie so that he could see my stomach. It wasn't big yet, but I was showing enough for him to tell I was pregnant.

"Damn, Babe..." He reached and touched my belly. "That's crazy!"

I was scared to know what he was going to say. Terrified of how he felt. "Are you happy?" I asked, somewhat urgently.

All Marcus could do at first was nod. "Yeah... Yeah, I'm happy," he said finally. "A little shocked, but happy fa sho."

I was relieved to know that we would be doing this together. I would make sure Marcus never knew the truth after that look in his eyes. Don't judge me, I was just doing what I had to do. I didn't want to hurt him.

Before we could finish talking, his family started walking in. I whispered in his ear to keep the baby between us, just until he got out of there. He agreed and kissed me on my cheek. I spoke to his mama and sisters before I left. I let everyone know I'd be back later. I was going to let him spend time with his people.

▪▪

All I know is play for keeps, I ain't slept in 'bout a week

Niggas screamin' we got beef, shell casings in the street

You gon' ride or die, you gon' ride or die

—*Lil Baby*

CHAPTER 24

Things have been going good for me lately . Me and Zay has been in a good space. The night he was supposed to come to my job, Passion ended up not coming to work, so everything worked out. To tell the truth, I had not talked to—or seen—Passion in a long time. It had been about a month, actually. At first, I was happy that she had left me alone, but for her not to be showing up for work was weird. I would call her later to see what was up with her.

I was on my way to meet Zay at his warehouse. It was count day, and since his spot was hit and Marcus got shot, he was very careful about how he was moving. Zay didn't know who to trust, so he only let me and Kwame help with count.

I pulled up to the warehouse, and to my surprise, I didn't see Zay's truck. That was weird, because he told me two hours ago that he was on his way there. I pulled out my phone and facetimed him. No answer. I called him the regular way and *still* no answer.

I didn't have time to be playing games with him. It seemed like every time we were doing good, he did some silly shit to piss me off. I sent him a text.

'Zay- Im here where u at ???'

The text showed as delivered, so I gave him a few minutes to respond. About ten minutes went past, and Kwame was pulling up. I got out of my truck to greet him. “Hey Kwame, you talked to Zay? I’ve been waiting on him for about twenty minutes...”

“No, I been calling him. No answer,” Kwame admitted.

I was beginning to worry now. “That’s not like him not to answer the phone for you, Kwame,” I explained. “Now, he might not answer for me, but for him not to answer for you? That’s not like him.”

Kwame stopped fumbling with the door’s lock. “Yeah, B, you right,” he nodded. “He always answers, and he knew today was count day, so I can’t see what could’ve been going on that he wouldn’t be here, or at least call or answer the phone.”

I was scared. So much had been going on these past few weeks that it made all kinds of stuff start running through my head. “Come on, B,” Kwame said, interrupting my panic. “Come in, we going start count and then go from there.”

He tuned on the light, and I couldn’t believe what I saw. Zay was beat so badly his left eye had swollen shut, and he was tied to a chair in the middle of the warehouse. I ran to untie him, screaming and crying. How could someone do this to him?

“What the fuck happened?!” Kwame demanded.

“I’m good!” Zay stated.

He wasn’t good, though, his face was truly fucked up. I couldn’t believe my eyes. “Who did this to you?!” I demanded, desperate for answers.

"I don't know," Zay replied, shaking his head. "I was getting out of my truck to come in and get ready to do count. Next thing I know, someone comes up from behind and hit me with their gun and put a bag over my head." My eyes went wide. "I blacked out, but I do remember it was three guys. Two of them were carrying me in, and the other one was giving out orders. The voices didn't sound familiar at all."

While listening to the disturbing story, I cleaned Zay up as best as I could. I helped him put on a clean shirt, we locked the warehouse up, and immediately went to the honeycomb hideout. It was a small condo out in Newport, so no one knew about this place but me and Kwame.

Once inside, we could finally talk. The condo was soundproof. Even if someone was outside the windows, they couldn't hear what we were discussing.

"Dawg, what the fuck. Whoever did this was trying to leave a message, because they didn't take nothing," said Kwame as he poured himself a drink. "No money, no product. Nothing."

That made things even worse. At least if they had taken something, we would have known exactly what kind of 'message' they were trying to send. "So y'all don't have no idea who could be doing this to y'all?" I asked. "First Li'l Marcus is shot, then **all** your spots, and now you in the warehouse tied up." I stared at the two of them with a serious look in my eye. "Somebody out to get y'all. Y'all need to figure out who it is, and fast!"

"Man, who you telling?" Zay curled up his lip. "I can't afford this shit! If you must know, the shit that's happen right now is fucking with my money! And you know how I get when people fuck with my money."

We all nodded in agreement, but he just continued ranting. "Now, at first, I thought the **Lil Marcus** situation was just some young niggas trying to get off, but then our spot gets hit? That shit just blew me away, I never been in this situation in all the years I've been hustling." Zay lowered his head, holding it in both his palms. "I *know* Niggas, . They're never betrayed me, so I know there's got to be somebody new or somebody who don't know how I get down, but I got to put an end to this shit."

We sat there and kicked it for about three more hours, and we could come up with no conclusion on who was fucking with them. I had to be to work in a few hours, so I cooked Zay something to eat and told him I would be back after my shift.

I knew he was going to chill there for a few days until he healed up a little. I also needed to check up on my little sister. Maybe Marcus had told her what happen the day he got shot and he could help put some of the puzzle pieces of what was going on together. I kissed Zay goodbye and left.

It took me about thirty minutes to make it home. I had only two hours before I had to be to work. I felt bad knowing he would have to shut down for about a month. Yeah, we had money put up—more than enough to live off of for a few years at least, but it's always best to make more. At least, I know *I* loved having my own money, and if something went bad, I was gonna have to take care of him just like he took care of me when I didn't have much.

Neither one of my sisters were there when I got to the house, so I went upstairs to my room and hopped in the shower. By the time I got out, I had two missed calls from Passion. I wonder what she wanted? I haven't talked to her or even seen her in a while, and I knew she was in her feelings because I was curving her.

I guess now she's over it. She hadn't even been at work in a while, and I was doing **My show** cases with this other girl named Desire. I hoped Passion didn't show up at work on any kind of bullshit. Her and Desire did not get along at all. That's all I needed was for some more bullshit to jump off.

Holding me tight

Loving me right

Giving me life

All night

You could be (You could be)

Telling me lies

Making me cry

Wasting my time

The whole time

So just be

Careful what you take for granted, yeah

'Cause with me know you could do damage

-Her

CHAPTER 25

BRAZIL

It seemed like as soon as things started looking up for us, something else happened. Marcus had woken up and was doing good, but Zay's warehouse just got hit. I wonder if that and what happened to Marcus is connected? Kwame was tripping, because he felt like he should've been there.

I had just gotten to the shop myself, and I had eight heads today. Kwame wanted me to stay with him, but I couldn't—I was booked up. He offered to pay me for the day, but I insisted that I couldn't. I know, right? He's toxic as hell. I had been spending a lot of time with him lately; he was just so nice to me. I couldn't wrap my mind around it. He was actually a nice guy.

I was washing my client's head, and I heard a lot of commotion coming from the front of the shop. I didn't pay it any mind until I heard someone yell my name. I walked to the front to see what was going on. It was Ron, arguing with the front desk assistance.

"Ron!" I snapped. "What are you doing here?"

His face was red; he was furious. I didn't care. "So, you fucking with that nigga Kwame, Zil?! And don't lie to me, because I seen you with him at the mall!" Ron yelled at me.

"First of all, lower your voice, Ron," I demanded, disgusted. "I don't know who you think you talking to or why you're checking about what I got going on in my life. I'm no longer your concern."

"What you mean, Zil?" he asked as if he had forgotten entirely what he had been doing. Wouldn't be surprising if he did, considering he already forgot me telling him to shut his mouth and keep his voice down. "You will always be my concern—I love you!"

It made me feel sick to my stomach. "Listen," I began, icily. "It's been over between us, okay? You didn't love me when you were fucking with every bitch that would show you some attention, so *please* leave, Ron."

I was getting irritated with him now. He was at my job, putting on a show for God and everyone. I should have just stayed home, I didn't have time for this. I had hair to do, and Ron was throwing me off. "Ron, can you please leave?" I repeated. "This is my job. You are acting really crazy right now, and I don't have time for these games you're playing."

"I'm not playing, Brazil!" he exploded, his voice raising despite my attempts to stop it. "I love you and I'm sorry for everything I did! Can you please just talk to me? I'm not leaving until you talk to me. You won't answer any of my calls, you blocked me on all social media, this is the only way I can talk to you!" Ron pleaded.

I grit my teeth. "Ron, I blocked you because you were spamming my page. I told you we were done, and I have nothing else to say to you!" I snarled. "You hurt me for the last time. We don't need to talk—there is nothing else to talk about—you should just *move on.* I'm done. Now can you *please* leave before there's a problem?!" I was yelling at this point. I was fed up with him.

Now he stopped sniveling and moved back to anger again. “Oh, what’s the problem going be, huh? You going call your little gangsta boyfriend?” He began to walk up on me. “That’s what you going to do, huh?”

As soon as he got close to me, Kwame walked in, and I felt so embarrassed I could have died on the spot. “She not going have to call me, because I’m already here,” Kwame said.

“Shit, please, Kwame, I got this,” I urged as he wrapped his arms around me. The last thing I wanted was a bloodbath at my job. “Ron, please leave,” I asked him once more. I didn’t want it to go any further.

Ron had other ideas. “Listen, Zil, I just want to talk to you, and you acting like a *BITCH* because you fucking this nigga!” he screamed.

Before I could respond, Kwame punched him in the mouth. “You mad disrespectful, my dogg,” he noted coldly.

Ron tried to fight back, but he couldn’t fuck with Kwame, and Kwame threw Ron right out the front door. “It’s not over!” Ron yelled as he walked to his car.

I can’t believe that all this happened at my place of work. I was so embarrassed; I hate that this had to happen here. “Kwame what are you doing here?” I asked him, eager to get my mind off of what I had seen.

He gave a light laugh. “I came to bring you some food,” he said, rubbing the back of his neck sheepishly. “I knew you had a full book today and wouldn’t have time to get anything. I guess I came right on time, huh?

My face still felt totally hot. “Yeah, I guess, but you didn’t have to do that! I was going to get him to leave,” I insisted.

“Well, he was disrespecting my girl. I couldn’t have that,” Kwame sweetly replied as he kissed me on my cheek. His touched gave me chills. Before, I was just so mad at everything that went on, but as soon as he wrapped his arms around me, all my anger went out the window; it was like I was in a daze. “How many people you got left, Baby?”

“Four more people, and I’m behind because of all the bullshit that just happened,” I sighed, rolling my eyes. “I’ll be here till, like, ten PM, and I hate staying that late,” I explained as I placed my client under the dryer.

He wrapped his arm around me in a quick hug. “Well, Baby, I’mma go grab you something to eat and go to take care of some business. I’ll be here to pick you up by nine thirty,” Kwame responded.

“Aww, you don’t have do that, I’ll be fine,” I cooed, kissing him on the cheek. “Plus, I want to go home tonight and see my sisters. I been with you every night for the past week. I know they miss me, and I need to check on Bianca.”

“Girl, please,” he laughed. “I’ll be here to pick you up and then *WE* can go check on your sister.” Before I could say anything, he kissed me on my lips and told me he would see me later.

■■■

The Risks We Take for Love

Mama, I'm a stepper, I can't walk by fate

Every day, I wake up to some brand-new hate

Every nigga opps, every nigga wants some, it's on everybody top

All these storms that I weathered, most couldn't take

I got problems with some niggas 'cause I won't be fake

Every nigga opps, every nigga wants some, it's on everybody top

—Fredo Bang

CHAPTER 26

Kwame

The shit that was going on right now was crazy. We had to shut down everything until we figured out who had a hit out on us. I couldn't put my thumb on it, because we really weren't beefing with anyone for real. I know for a fact that Ron nigga couldn't be the one behind all this that was happening. I needed to go kick it with Zay to see where he thought this was coming from.

I pulled up to the hideout where Zay had been staying. It was best that he stay out the way, after all. We needed to call a meeting, but was afraid, because we didn't know where these hits were coming from. We could only trust each other right now.

It was like Fort Knox trying to get into the grounds. It took me twenty minutes before I was even pushing the code into the front door. "What up, Nigga?" I greeted, locking up with Zay.

He was on the couch, watching TV. Or, staring through it, really. "Shit. Nothing, my baby, just chilling trying to get my thoughts together." He laughed without much humor.

I nodded. "I feel you on that. There's so much going on, it's hard to think about where this shit is coming from," I agreed as I poured myself a shot.

"I really need to talk to Marcus to see what he remembers from the night he got shot. He woke up the other day, B told me he should be home in a week or two," Zay said as he got up and walked into the kitchen.

"I know, Zil was telling me she wanted to stay at home tonight so she could kick it with her sister. Little do she know im staying with her too," I snickered with a smile on my face. I was really feeling Zil and found myself thinking about her all day, it was crazy as hell.

"Damn, my nigga. Let girly breathe," Zay replied, laughing.

I couldn't help it; I guffawed. "I know you ain't talking. You be up B's ass, you scared she going leave you with all the fucked-up shit you be doing to sis."

"Boy, chill out! B ain't leaving me, nigga, no matter what," he insisted, and that just made me roll my eyes. Of course, he felt that way. Brittany hadn't left him for good yet.

"That's your problem—you think she won't leave your ass," I noted as I pulled my phone out to text Zil.

Zay wasn't acting too offended, he kept talking like I hadn't said anything. "So listen, Cuz. I need you to keep your ears to the streets," he encouraged. "Go kick it with Marcus and I'll call Javier, check in, let him know what's going on and that we taking care of it... You know how he is. As soon as he thinks we can't handle it, he gets to tripping." Boy did I know it.

"This ain't nothing we can't take care of, so let's just get it handled," Zay finished.

I looked up from my phone. "How we going get something handled and you sitting up in here watching movies and eating popcorn? I mean I know you had to get yourself together, but I need you out here with me, Cuz, its only right," I pointed out, staring him down. "You might as well get dressed so we can get out here and handle this shit."

I know he had just got his ass beat, but I mean, he was good. It was time to get shit in order, and fast. We had shut down, and yeah, we were good money-wise, but we had workers who couldn't just sit on their asses doing nothing for too long.

His face went from irate to thoughtful. "You right," he agreed eventually. "I'm 'bout to get some shit in order and have B come get me in a few hours," Zay said as he stood up to go upstairs.

I chilled for a little while, then I told Zay I would meet him at the girls' house later on. I had a few things I wanted to handle before I went in for the day. I hate having to leave Zil, so I tried my best to try to handle everything I needed to do beforehand.

I didn't think me and Zil would click as fast as we did. I mean I had been chasing her for ages, but I never thought she would give me the time of day like this. I know y'all might think she was only fucking with me because that lame-ass nigga played her, but she was feeling me before then, and I know it. That day I helped her study, I knew then.

I was really into her, and I wasn't going to fuck this up. I am willing to change everything for her. I wasn't any type of wild nigga, but I did fuck with a few hoes, and since I had been fucking with Zil, those hoes were mad about it. Calling and texting me all kinds of stuff. But fuck them, I'm off their asses. Well—for now, anyway.

I had just pulled back up in the hood, it was pretty dead around here since we closed up shop. We ran every corner in the city, so when we shut down, the city shut down. I pulled into the gas station a couple of blocks from our first trap house. We still had the house, but we didn't run anything out of it anymore. It was just a little chill spot we let our young dogs chill at and sell their weed out of it.

I walked into the gas station, and there was a boy that was about seventeen, sitting on the corner next to the coffee machine. "What up, big homie, you smoke? I got some ZAZAs," the little dude asked me.

"What? Naw, nigga, I don't want no ZAZAs, and who the fuck you selling for on my block?" I asked him with a frown on my face. I had never seen this boy before, so how the fuck was he selling weed on my corners.

"What?" he parroted. "Chill out. You all in my business, who the fuck is you? The police?" He asked as he jumped down.

I laughed at him. "Oh, you don't know who I am? Yet you on my block selling your little weed. Yeah, you can't be from around here."

"All you had to say was 'naw, I don't smoke' and keep it moving, my dog," he said with a little groan.

He was talking so recklessly. I couldn't imagine who he was working for that had him feeling like he was 'The Man'.

"Listen, tell me who the fuck you working for before I kill you right here." I said, grinding the bottom of my shoe on the ground in anger.

"You going have to kill me my nigga, I ain't telling you shit," he said, not even blinking twice, and continued talking, "These my blocks now, so you going have to do what you got to do." He smirked, crossing his arms over his chest.

This was crazy to me. Here I was, thinking 'should I kill this tough ass kid for talking crazy? For working on my block?' He had no fear in his heart at all.

I smacked him in the mouth with the butt of my gun.

"Listen, little boy, tell whoever sent you over here on my block to sell anything that they just signed your death certificate." I pointed my Glock in between his eyes

"Listen dog, you tripping! I was just trying to make a few dollars, you ain't got to kill me!" the little boy cried out.

I wasn't going to kill him, but he didn't know that. The little nigga's tears were running down his face and snot was dripping from his nose. "Listen, you going to tell me who you working for, and then I don't want to see you around here no more. You understand me!?" I demanded as I grabbed him up by his shirt.

"Look man, his name's Tommy. I don't know too much about him, I just know me, and my boys was at the park and he rode up on us. Then he asked if we wanted to work for him, and he said we could keep forty percent. Me and my boys jumped on it 'cause we was broke, and that was it. Can you please let me go, man!? Please, I promise you will never see me again!" He cried his little heart out.

I smacked him with the butt of my gun and let him go. He ran as soon as I let him go.

Fuck, man. Today went all the way left. I called Zay to ask if he had ever heard of anybody named Tommy. He was just as clueless as me. He was on his way to the hood and was going meet me at the girls' house. I took the video from the camera from the clerk and walked out of the gas station.

I hopped in my black-on-black Scat and pulled off. I can't wait till everything is back to normal. I was taking me and Zil on a trip I needed to clear my mind.

▪▪

Fuckin' Robitussin
I don't know why this shit got me lazy right now, yeah
Can't do Percocets or Molly
I'm turnin' one, tryna live it up here right, right, right

-Chris Brown

▪▪▪

CHAPTER 27

I bet you guys thought I wasn't going to get to say my part and give my side of the story. Well, you're all wrong, and here it goes.

I had been calling and texting Brittany, and still no answer. I heard that she was doing our stage show with Desire. I couldn't believe her. I figured that I would show up at work tonight just so she would have to dance with me.

I had stopped dancing for real. I had let her throw me off my square. If I showed up to work, then she would have no choice but to do the set with me. Then I could talk to her. I know she's back fucking with my sister's baby-daddy because that's the only time she would ignore me.

She did say we were going stop doing what we were doing, but I didn't think she was being for real. I had fallen in love with her, and I wondered why she couldn't see that. She really needed to leave Zay alone. He wasn't good for her. I was who she needed. I know she loved how I made her feel, and Zay was still fucking my sister whenever he wanted to.

"Passion, Passion!" Krystal called my name from the other room.

"What, Krystal!? Damn!" I yelled back, walking into the living room to see what she wanted.

"You want a bump?" Krystal asked me as she wiped her nose.

"Yeah, I do bitch. So, you been in here getting high and just now thought to ask if I wanted some?" I bent down to snort the line off the glass table. "Bitch, where'd you get this from?" I asked, wiping my nose off.

"I got it from my homegirl at work. You know its dry around here ever since BD and them shut down." Krystal said, shifting around a bit.

"Girl, you should've told her to keep that shit. You know how much of that I need to feel something? Whoever your homegirl got that from, she stepped on that shit too hard," I scoffed.

I walked back into my room and picked up my phone. I was checking to see if Brittany called, and of course she didn't. It had been weeks since I heard from her. I had to get her to talk to me, so I sent her another text.

I had been getting so high lately, that's why I hadn't been working. I had been partying with my sister. Tonight, however, I was going in. I had to see Brittany, *I had to.* I was going to show up to work and we were going to do our show and turn up like always. Yeah, that's what I was going do. I knew if I showed up, Shawn was going make Brittany do the stage show with me. We always made the niggas throw the most money. The more money we made, the more money he made.

I called Brittany again to see if she would answer. She didn't answer. I called back again, and I couldn't believe it.

She picked up. "What's up, P?" She said in that sweet voice. The sound of her voice made my panties wet.

"Hey Baby, what's up? I been calling you and texting you and getting no response." I asked, trying not to sound upset.

"Yeah, I been having a lot going on, P. What you want though? I'm bout to get ready for work," she asked back.

"I want you, B. We ain't chilled in a while." I really was hoping she was down.

"Listen, P. I told you I wasn't feeling that shit no more." She said, sounding irritated.

"Brittany don't do that. Let's just talk about it tonight." I begged. "We used to have so much fun, you know you miss me" I continued pleading.

"Passion, I got to go. Zay just pulled up." Then she hung up.

I was so mad. She really was playing me for that nigga Zay. I couldn't believe her. After all Zay did to her and put her through, she was still willing to be with him. I tried to get Krystal to call and try to fuck Zay. However, she was so far up her new nigga's ass that she wasn't paying him any mind. I had a plan. If going to work tonight to see Brittany didn't work, I was putting it in motion.

I loved her, and what I was about to do was going to be for us. She'd understand once it was all over. I hated that she was bringing out this side of me. I didn't want to have to show her my bad side. In the end, everything would fall in place. Me and Brittany were going to be together, and I'd make sure of that.

I took out my plate and snorted three lines. Then I started getting ready for work.

Wanna break down but I can't, I gotta hold up
Wanna free my mind but I'm tryna stay sober
I ain't really live yet, I'm only gettin' older

I got too much to say (ooh-ooh)
Yeah, I got too much to say (oh-oh)
I got too much I have (woah-oh)
I got too much to say (oh-oh, ooh)

-Queen Naija

CHAPTER 28

BIANCA

I was so happy that Marcus had woken up, and that I was able to tell him about the baby. It was like as soon as I told him about the baby, his whole mood changed. He was doing everything he could to get out of the hospital.

I had just got back up to his room, and the whole hood was up there now seeing him. It was packed. I didn't feel like dealing with all this. I was going to tell Marcus that I would be back later when it died down. I walked up to his bedside, and he was up, talking to a few of our friends "Hey Baby, what's up?" I cooed as I walked over and kissed him on the cheek.

"Nothing, Baby. I was waiting on you to get back up here so I can kick all these niggas out," he laughed.

"You don't got to kick nobody out, I'll come back later. I know they want to see you, bae, you been out for like a month," I assured him.

"Fuck these niggas, I am trying to chill with you," he protested, frowning.

"Bae, it's cool. I know y'all got stuff to talk about." I said as I reached for my phone. It had been ringing nonstop since I got here. I checked the caller ID, and it was *KIM.* I had been ignoring her ever since she played me. I was the only one who wanted to give her a chance, but now I see why my sisters don't fuck with her. All I needed was for her to sign a fucking paper and she charged me and still didn't want to show up. I ignored the call, and let it ring until it eventually stopped.

I wanted to go home and kick it with my sisters. We all have been doing our own thing and haven't spent much time together. There was so much going on in our lives right now.

I sat there while Marcus kicked with his boys. It was about three hours later, and everybody was gone. I was finally able to talk to him alone. "So, how you feeling? I know you're going to say you're okay, but you can keep it real with me. I want to know how you feel about being shot."

"I mean I am mad as fuck. I can't believe I let a hoe-ass nigga get me. Soon as I get out of here though, I'm gonna handle it," Marcus reassured himself while sitting up a little.

"Listen Marcus, I know you want to get them. You need to think about us. You can't imagine how it feels having to sit by your hospital bed waiting for you to wake up." I pleaded with him.

I was going lay it on thick. I needed Marcus to get out of the game, get a job, and to move me and the baby out of the hood. Yeah, I know what you're thinking. *'That's **might** not even **be** his baby!'* Whatever, I would never tell him the truth. I couldn't even tell my sisters whose baby it was. I had a plan, and I was going make sure it fell through.

"Bae, you know I think about you and the baby every day. I just can't up and leave the game like that. I'm a young nigga, and I just really started making money and proving myself. Ain't no way I'm going bitch up 'cause I got shot. I can't let niggas think they got off on me, hell naw." Marcus picked his phone up from the side table and began texting someone.

I knew I had made him mad, but oh well. I had to put it in his ear about leaving, so that he could at least think about it. I didn't want to raise a child here. I mean yes, I do have my sisters, but there's really nothing here for me. Look at everything that's going on. It was just too much.

I stayed with Marcus for a few hours, and we just kicked it. The doctors were saying he might be able to come home in a week.

I was pulling up at home. I needed to lay back with my friends for a little while before my sisters got home, because I had been spinning Carlos and Kimmy. I really didn't want to talk to them about everything that was going on, and Kimmie was kind of judging me since I told her I was keeping my baby.

Carlos had been supporting me the whole time, and I don't really know why I was acting funny towards him. I decided that I would reach out to him. Truth be told, I needed somebody to talk to that wasn't my sisters. Sure, they were over the fact that I was having a baby, but still they weren't all for it yet. I just needed to talk to someone who was team Bianca no matter what.

Me: Hey Los I know I been
ghosting you, but I want to
chill and catch up. I been going

through a lot wanted to let you know it's nothing you did. Actually, you have been there for me the whole time.

💪**Los BFF**💗**:** What's up Bebe I was wondering what was going on, but umm I'm busy today maybe we can link this weekend. Cool??

Me: Sure, that's cool just let me kno

💪**Los BFF**💗**:** Bet

I put my phone down next to me and got my stuff ready for my shower. I knew my sisters would be home soon and I wanted to chill before they got here.

My phone went off and I picked it up. It was my mom calling me for the thousandth time. I don't know what she wanted, and I wasn't trying to find out. I had washed my hands with her for how she played me. I sent her call to voicemail and continued to get ready for my bath.

By the time I got out of the tub I could hear my sister downstairs talking. I went downstairs to chill with them. "Hey Bebe." Zil said, looking up from her phone.

"Hey sissy." I said as I sat next to B on the couch.

"How are you feeling? Is the baby, okay?" Brittany asked me.

"I'm good, and the baby is fine. It's a girl, and I found out last week," I replied back to her.

"OMG, Bebe! You're just now saying something?" Zil squealed, getting up to hug me.

I didn't think they would be so happy, but I guess they are getting ready to love the baby just like they loved me. It put me at ease a little. "Yeah, Bebe, I can't wait to plan this baby shower. We need some happiness around here after all we been through." Brittany said.

"I don't know if I'm having one," I admitted.

"Girl, is you crazy? This our first niece. We having a big ass baby shower," Zil insisted as she stood up and walked out of the room.

It was crazy how mad they were at first, and now they want to give me a baby shower. I just figured they meant they would support me through whatever. I hope they really do support me through everything, because I know they would eventually want to know who my baby's daddy really was.

Brittany wasn't dumb, she knew I wasn't fucking with Marcus like that. She even mentioned it to me when I first told her. I just brushed it off, but I knew she would bring it back up sooner or later. I mean, I'm going tell them. I just don't know when or how. I guess I'll figure it out when the time comes. When they knew the truth, it was going to cause a lot of problems and we didn't need that right now.

■■

The Risks We Take for Love

Hope you never find out who I really am
'Cause you'll never love me,
You'll never love me, you'll never love me
But I believe you when you say it like dat
Oh, do you mean it when you say it like dat?
Oh, I believe you when you say it like dat
You must really love me

—SZA

CHAPTER 29

It was the first time in a while that all of us were at home just chilling. I missed this. It hadn't been just the three of us at home together in a while. I mean, we were always in and out. I was working, and when I wasn't, I was with Zay at the hideout. Zil has been staying with Kwame, and Bebe was back and forth at the hospital. Things had been crazy for the past few weeks, and stuff was just starting to chill out.

Passion was still being crazy. I did my best to avoid her, but I knew it wasn't going to last for long. I had even switched to dayshift just so I didn't have to see her. Sure, I wasn't making as much money, but I was doing little runs for Zay since he shut down, so it was cool for now.

Speaking of Zay, he and Kwame had just walked in and were rolling up a blunt. I was in the kitchen making some turkey chops, while Zil mixed up some green tea shots. It felt kind good to be all together again. Yeah, there was still a lot of stuff that needed to be taken care of and figured out, but we weren't going worry about that tonight; I was just trying to enjoy time with them.

Passion had been calling my phone back-to-back all day and I had to put it on Do Not Disturb. I should've never messed with her. I know I was wrong, but she was cool at first. The only issue was that once I told her our relationship was just for fun, it's like she went crazy.

We both knew that what we were doing was wrong, but we did it anyway. Like, shit, she was Zay's baby mama's sister, how fucked up was that? Oh well, what's done is done. I promised myself to tell Zay one day, because things with her were getting out of hand. I remember him telling me that Krystal and Passion's mom was bipolar, and I'm starting to see signs of it in her.

We had been chilling for a few hours now. Me and Zay were in a good space for once. The two of us were sitting at the table playing cards, while Bebe watched a movie, and Kwame and Zil sat together on the love seat. I was really happy for Brazil—she was finally coming out her shell! I never though her and Kwame would be kicking it like they were. I guess it took a heartbreak to open herself up to the idea.

My phone buzzed. It was Zay texting me from across the table.

Zay😶🥓🤞: Lets go upstairs real quick

Me: Boyyyy Go head on

Zay😶🥓🤞: Stop playing B

Me: Oh, you want some of this good pussy huh

Zay😶🌊✌️: You know I do,
I'm all healed up now

Me: 🤪🤪🤪

I got up and walked up the stairs to my room, and Zay was right behind me. It had been a while since we fucked, and I missed him a ton. The second we walked in my bedroom, he pushed me up against the door, and started laying kisses all over me and let his rough hands explore my body. I pulled his V-neck T-shirt over his head, then took off my Nike sports bra, and my perky brown breasts sat up just right.

He grabbed my chocolate chip nipples and pulled them in his mouth; he knew that was the way to turn me up. He sucked on the buds while tugging my biker shorts down with his other hand. "Oh, so you just out here wearing biker shorts with no panties, huh?" he snickered while still moving his mouth to my other nipple.

I tried to shoot a glare at him. "Boy, shut up, I just got out the tub before you got here," I moaned. He took his hand and gripped my ass, using it to slide me in closer to him so we could begin to kiss passionately. This is what I missed. I miss the love we had when we first started dating. No fighting, no baby mama drama—just me and my man. As we made out, he began to rub my clit, only to pop his lips free from mine and placed my breast back into his mouth.

I began to slip into a daze. My heart was pounding, and I was about to cum. "Yesss, Xavier! Don't stop—" I whispered in his ear.

"Oh, you like that, huh, Baby? You called me by my government." Zay knew it was real when I called him by his actual name. He rubbed my clit so gentle, then he inserted two fingers, and oh my God, that almost took me over the edge.

I was trying my hardest not to cum yet—I wanted to enjoy the trip. I knew this was going to be a long night. I was just trying to get a quicky, but the way things were going, I had a feeling that wasn't going to be the case.

■■

I'm going down

'Cause I know that it's you I see in my dreams

I'm going down

Let me drown over you living in my dream

(In my dreams)

—Ella Mae

CHAPTER 30

I finally was at home chilling with my sisters. Of course, Kwame and Zay were here, but still. It felt good to be back doing what we normally did. We had eaten well, had a few drinks, and were just kicking it. B and Zay went upstairs about an hour ago, and Bebe was asleep on the couch.

I had finally faced the fact that my baby sister was having a baby. I wanted so much more for her, but I guess I couldn't write her story for her. Instead, I would continue to help her and support her no matter what. She looked so peaceful just lying there with her little baby bump. I was so glad Marcus had pulled through. She didn't need to be out here raising a baby by herself. I covered my sister up with a blanket and turned off the light.

Kwame was going to stay the night with me. He made sure all the doors were locked and we went to my room. I was really feeling him; he was nothing like I thought he would be. He was showing me stuff I never experienced before and truly making me fall for him.

I had been with him every day since that night at the club. We still haven't had sex yet, and he wasn't pressuring me. I think that's why I liked him so much—he didn't make me feel uncomfortable. I mean, we messed around a little, but it never went any farther than that.

I was sprawled across my bed in a robe waiting on my grades to post, while Kwame was next to me, watching TV.

The energy between us was so lit; It was like we were in sync together.

I kept refreshing my computer, and nothing.

He sucked his teeth, and I glanced over at him. "Damn, Baby. Put the computer up and watch this movie with me," Zay said as he pulled me closer to his side.

"I can't Kwame, I have to see if I passed!"

Kwame rolled his eyes. "Now, you know you passed. Stop stressing, Bae, lets chill," he insisted as he closed my laptop

I gasped. "Oh my God, Kwame, why would you do that?!" I whined as I mushed his face. "I won't be able to sleep until I know what my grade is, you know how important it is that I pass this class!"

"Here, let me take your mind off it just for a minute..." he murmured as he pulled me in and pressed our lips together; I had chills through my body every time his skin made contact with mine.

He untied my robe and pulled it off, revealing the black lace panties and bra I was wearing. His hands crested my thighs as he kissed me deep, and I was feeling something I never felt before. I didn't want to take it all the way there yet with him, but I didn't want him to stop either.

As we made out, his hands slid up my back to unhook my bra, causing my perky C-cup breasts to fall out. He took the opportunity to grab one and roll my nipple between his fingers, while I began to kiss him harder. His touch felt so good.

He was laying on top of me looking so *fine.* His dreads hung down and brushed across my chest as he pulled my breast into his mouth. The warmth of his mouth took me to a place I had never been. At least, back during that night at the club, I was so drunk, but I don't ever remember it feeling like this. As he continued to suck my breast, moving from one to the next, he slipped his hand near my panty line. I tensed up.

"If you want me to stop, I will, bae," he whispered.

"No, no, no, please don't stop," I breathlessly begged, trying to compose myself.

He slipped my panties down and flipped me over. "You know, I will stop if it's beginning to be too much..." I can't believe I was laying here ass-naked just letting him have his way with me.

When I looked over my shoulder, he was grabbing the oil from my dresser, which he used to begin to massage my whole body. He rubbed me from head to toe, then came back up and parted my legs.

So much was going through my head. Was I really about to fuck him? Was I ready? As good as this felt, did I want to lose my virginity right now—to him?

While I was thinking of all these things, I felt his wet, warm tongue on my clit, and he started eating my pussy so good I thought my eyes would roll back into my head. I was cumming back-to-back, and he just kept going.

Yeah, I think I was ready for the real thing. I wasn't going to tell him, but if he tried, I'd let him go all the way. He slipped up to be face-to-face with me and pressed in a quick smooch, and when he pulled his underwear down, and what I saw made my mouth water. Oh my God, was this normal? Like, was I supposed to feel like this?

"Baby, are you sure you ready?" he murmured as he peppered kisses down my neck and collarbone, across my jaw, to the cheek, then finishing on my lips.

I rolled my head back on stack of pillows I had on my bed . "Yes, Kwame, I'm ready, but don't hurt me, okay?" I softy responded.

I can't believe I was really about to do this. I was ready though—ready to feel the real thing. Sure, I loved getting head, but I knew that the real thing had to feel better. "You know I wouldn't hurt you. If you want me to stop, just tell me."

After that, Kwame was pecking me with kisses again and rubbing his hands all over my body, eating my pussy and rolling my clit with his thumb at the same time. I came so hard I was dizzy. He popped back up to rest on top of me and I felt him put the tip in. As it stretched the opening, I felt a burning feeling, and I pulled back.

"You okay?" he asked. "Want me to stop?"

I shook my head. "No, go ahead," I assured him as I leaned my head back and just waited for him to ease it in. He gently pushed a little bit more, and my eyes squeezed shut.

BOOM.

I heard glass break. Kwame jumped up. *BOOM.* More glass broke, and then, Brittany screamed. **BOOM.** My room's window broke, and glass went everywhere, allowing the room to fill with smoke.

The first thing I thought about was my baby sister sleeping downstairs. *I had to get to her.* I tried to run to the door, but it was so smoky, I couldn't see anything but flames beginning to form around me. I couldn't breathe—the smoke was too thick, so I tried my hardest to get out the room. I had to get to my sisters. I was trying to move, but my body felt heavy.

Then everything went **black.**

TO BE CONTINUED

Made in the USA
Middletown, DE
05 January 2023

21483344R00126